LLAMA UNITED

Cardiff Libraries
www.cardiff.gov.uk/libraries

Llyfrgelloedd Caerdydd
www.caerdydd.gov.uk/llyfrgelloedd

MACMILLAN CHILDREN'S BOOKS

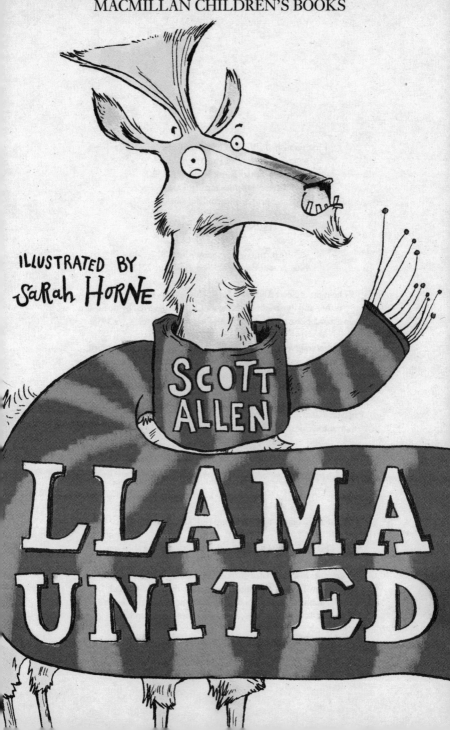

ILLUSTRATED BY
SaRah HORNE

SCOTT ALLEN

LLAMA UNITED

First published 2017 by Macmillan Children's Books
an imprint of Pan Macmillan
20 New Wharf Road, London N1 9RR
Associated companies throughout the world
www.panmacmillan.com

ISBN 978-1-5098-4090-8

1 3 5 7 9 8 6 4 2

A CIP catalogue record for this book is available from
the British Library.

Printed and bound by CPI Group (UK) Ltd, Croydon CR0 4YY

To Dad – sorry you missed it

PROLOGUE

Well, hello there. I don't need to introduce myself do I? You'll know who I am already, won't you?

You don't?

OK, well for the few readers who *don't* know who I am I'll enlighten you. I'm Arthur Muckluck – the world's greatest footballer – EVER.

What do you mean you've never heard of me? I'm Arthur Muckluck: over fifty England caps, three Cup winners' medals, two Division One league titles and a World Cup winner. A creative genius, rocket quick, brilliant in the air, composed in front of goal and never scared to make crucial, crunching tackles. I even went in goal on two separate occasions – saved two penalties and kept two clean sheets. They used to call me 'The Legend' . . .

You remember me now, don't you?

No?! What do they teach you in school nowadays?

Don't you learn about the Golden Age of football? When footballs were as heavy as cannonballs, boots were made out of leather as thick as rump steaks, and football kits were exactly the same as the horrible chunky jumpers your gran knits for Christmas.

You don't have lessons about football at school? Oh.

Poor you.

ARTHUR MUCKLUCK

Well, this book isn't really about me – it's about some llamas, an eleven-year-old boy and some other random fruitcakes who wander into his life. I'm just going to help you along with the story, so you don't get bored.

Now, I might have been one of the world's greatest footballers, but this sadly didn't stop me having a fatal accident in my kitchen one Tuesday morning. I was doing some keepie-ups with a jar of mayonnaise, a plastic one not a glass one (I'm not stupid!), when I slipped on a slice of cheese that had boldly escaped from the fridge. I came crashing down and then . . . nothing.

I was a goner. The cheese and the mayonnaise also met a sticky end.

My wife, a lovely woman who happens to have rather hairy palms, thought it would be nice to scatter my ashes on the first field I ever played football on. The football historians among you will know this was in deepest darkest East London, where I grew up. Unfortunately, my wife is a bit forgetful, and she ended up in a field on a farm nearly three hundred miles away. Close-ish some might say. At least she got the country right.

It wasn't a particularly pleasant field; sitting on the outskirts of a small village, and full of weeds and discarded junk. At the time I wished she had picked a better place for me, to be honest. However, by sheer fluke, as you will find out later, she selected a field that plays a crucial role in the rest of this book. Round of applause for my wife . . . no? OK, let's move on.

Because of her hairy palms, as she attempted

to open the large black urn containing my ashes it slipped out of her grasp and cartwheeled away, scattering my mortal remains all over the grotty field before coming to a rest between a discarded pink sofa and a lime-green sink. The sink had retired there after thirty years in the army. I don't know where the sofa came from.

Are you still with me? Good, because this will be important later. For now, let's go and see what our hero, the eleven-year-old boy I mentioned earlier, is up to . . .

1
MEET THE GRAVYS

Frank Gravy looked out of the window. It was grey, cold and blustery outside. Through the murk he could see his eleven-year-old son, Chipsn, playing football in the puddles in the yard. Not really! He wasn't called Chipsn; that would mean he would be called Chipsn Gravy. What a stupid name that would be. Frank's son was actually called, rather boringly, Tim.

Tim was playing in the puddles on his own because he didn't have any friends. Two months ago he had lived in the city and had loads of friends at his school. But Frank had decided that he didn't want to work selling photocopier ink anymore and fancied becoming a farmer in the 'middle of nowhere'. Which is just next to 'I've never heard of it' and on the borders of 'I'm lost, where is this place again?' The family wasn't pleased with this sudden job change. It made them all really miserable. The kind of miserable you feel when you discover someone has forgotten to get the pigs-in-blankets for Christmas dinner.

Tim is eleven, average height, average build, average hair colour, average shoe size, average eye colour, average-sized nose, just average all round really. He would wrongly describe himself as 'all right' at everything. He was actually quite good at sport, quite good at English and quite good at computer games, but he always felt there was someone better than him. Tim didn't have the self-confidence to really push himself to be brilliant at anything. He took small parts in school plays, was the reserve keeper in the football team and was happy coming third or fourth in everything on sports day. Tim didn't really mind – he had some good friends and was fairly content with being an average sort of fellow. But that all changed when the Gravys left the city.

Tim's new school was tiny. It was attended by just twenty children and he was the only child in Year Six. Not only was he the eldest, but he was also the only child in the school with all his own teeth. This sounds odd doesn't it? But there is a good reason. Every summer, all the children have swimming lessons in the village pond. Large, dark and incredibly cooling in the hot summer months, it's also green, slimy and full of hidden nasties. The truth is, swimming in the mucky pond not only rots teeth, it isn't very good for the brain either. Not that the villagers have worked this out. They just think they all have bad teeth because the nearest dentist lives fifty miles away (and they have never even bothered to think about why they aren't very clever).

This made Tim, with his average teeth and average brain, stick out like a sore thumb. Every time the teacher asked Tim to answer an easy question, all the other children would laugh, point at his normal set of teeth and scoff at his cleverness. They also mocked his height, his age, his hair and even his choice of socks, which were usually just black. This went on every day for two months solid and made him thoroughly miserable. He was no longer average. Poor Tim; I do hope the rest of this story will make him a bit happier.

Tim has two very different sisters. Monica is seventeen and, if my maths is correct, the eldest of the Gravy children. She's a rarity when it comes to older sisters; incredibly cheerful, helpful, resourceful, intelligent, caring and brilliant with computers.

7

Luckily for Monica, she goes to college in the nearest town, which has a normal swimming pool. Although Monica doesn't really like swimming.

The youngest child is Fiona, and she is everything Monica isn't: annoying, loud, selfish and demanding. She's probably about six, and is prone to leaping out of cupboards and demanding sweets. Fiona goes to the same school as Tim but is incredibly popular because she is the only person with blonde hair. So unusual is her hair colour in the village, she is treated like a princess by her fawning classmates. She thinks this is brilliant and is

8

thinking of changing her name to 'The Lovely Fiona'.

Then comes Mum, or Beetroot as she is affectionately called by the rest of the family, because that's the colour she goes when she's been exercising. She used to be a dance instructor at an old people's home. There are hardly any old people's homes in the countryside and usually the last thing country folk want to do is learn how to twerk. She now spends her time making cakes and cookies and doing squat-thrusts. The farmhouse is bursting with tins and boxes full of sweet treats. There are only so many slices of cake you can eat in one day. Believe me I've tried. Ten pieces of Battenberg cake one teatime is my record. My sick was pink and yellow for a week.

Pets next? Nope, the Gravys have no pets, which is rare for a farming family. Tim had never understood what all the fuss was about having a pet. The prospect of picking up warm dog poo and putting it in a plastic bag made him shiver.

Then right at the back is Dad, or Frank as everyone is going to call him in this book, because hardly anyone is called Frank anymore and I think it's a name that needs a bit more glory. Most footballers in my day were called Clive or Frank or Roger . . . oh yes, or Pelo. No, not Pelé . . . what a foolish name.

Frank had sunk all of his money into the farm, which was horribly overpriced considering it only had two fields and one of them was full of rubbish. His other problem was that he knew absolutely nothing about being a farmer, expect for wearing wellingtons and occasionally leaning on fences to slowly give directions to people who were lost. This wouldn't be enough to keep a farm running. Farming is hard – as Frank and his family are about to find out.

2
THE BOY IN THE BUSH

Tim's walk to and from school wasn't particularly pleasant. To avoid the dangerous pavement-less road that the farm sat on, his classmates and his annoying younger sister, he had found a shortcut through the woods. It was a treacherous ten-minute scramble, but it was a small price to pay to avoid being teased before and after school.

On this particularly grotty Tuesday afternoon, Tim was making his way back from another thoroughly unfulfilling day at school, where he had, once again, learned nothing new. Being able to comfortably recite all the times tables up to twelve had left the rest of the class in fits of laughter for a good twenty minutes. Even the teacher was smirking at him. She had purple hair and carried a fish in her handbag, but no one ever commented on this or thought it was unusual. She could only do up to the three times table, and she really liked swimming in the village pond. Tim felt totally helpless. Spending five days a week in this school made him want to melt into a wall and become an untroubled, happy brick.

Tim had just grabbed a small, wet branch to stop himself sliding into a puddle as he negotiated the uneven path, when he noticed a pair of wellington boots sticking out from a thick bramble bush. One boot was green and the other was red, and they appeared to be attached to a pair of legs.

Tim approached with caution. The legs belonged to what looked like a boy of his age. The boy definitely didn't go to Tim's school, so he wondered where he had come from and what he was doing in the woods. The bramble bush looked really painful and Tim thought the boy must have tripped and fallen into it, probably knocking himself out in the process. His eyes were shut and his mouth was wide open.

Tim found a long, thin stick and poked the boy ever so gently in the stomach with it. Like you do with things you are not sure about. The boy didn't move. Perhaps he was dead, Tim thought, backing away.

Then, the boy suddenly let out the loudest snore ever and woke up.

He stared at Tim for a while from his thorny bed. 'Am I dead?' he asked in a rough but perky voice. He sounded like a local, but Tim had never seen him before.

'I don't think so,' said Tim, lowering the stick ever so slightly. He wasn't sure if this boy was going to be a threat. The stick was his only protection.

'Well, that's good isn't it? You never know what woodland creatures might have had a little nibble on you while you are trying to have a sleep, do you?'

Tim shrugged. He'd never wanted to sleep in a bramble bush, or even go camping for that matter. He liked his duvet and the nice, boiling-hot radiator in his bedroom at home too much.

The boy pulled himself out of the bush and stretched to his full height, which was exactly the same height as Tim. Tim took a step back and eyed him suspiciously. He was dressed like he had escaped from a charity shop. Above his mismatched wellies was a very battered pair of black tracksuit bottoms that had the word 'girlfriend' written in pink across the front. Clearly these were girls' tracksuit bottoms, and he was wearing them the wrong way round. On his body he wore what looked like chain mail over a computer game T-shirt. His face was fairly normal looking apart from the thin moustache he'd drawn in felt-tip pen above his top lip. His clump of black hair was full of twigs and looked like he'd just slept in a bush. Which he had.

'I'm Cairo, pleased to meet you,' said the boy, with a cheery wave.

Tim wasn't sure he had heard him correctly. He can't have said *Cairo*, his brain flickered curiously. Nobody is called Cairo.

'Hi Carl,' Tim's mouth said carefully. 'I'm Tim.' He casually tossed his stick into the nearest bush; this boy seemed friendly.

Cairo gave him a funny look and burst out laughing, showing a full set of normal white teeth. OK, some were a bit yellow round the edges, but whose aren't at eleven? Tim did a little inward sigh of relief. Clearly Cairo hadn't swum in the village pond.

'It's Cairo, not Carl. Like the capital of Egypt. *Cairo*.'

'Oh, sorry,' replied Tim politely. He desperately wanted to say 'Who the broken auntie is called Cairo?' and 'Are your parents a bit bonkers?' but decided that would be rude, especially to someone he'd just met.

'Don't worry,' the strangely dressed boy said with a grin. 'I get it all the time. My mum is a big fan of going on holiday. She loves Greece and wanted to call me Athens, but she got in a fluster when she was registering my name and blurted out Cairo instead. I'm glad, 'coz Athens is a girl's name.'

Tim frowned. He wasn't up to speed on which capital cities were girls' names and which weren't. 'Didn't your dad stop her?' he asked.

'Nah, I've never met him, and Mum doesn't really talk about him either. Means I can only get in trouble with one person I suppose.' Cairo smiled and did a tiny shrug. Tim wasn't great at reading people's feelings, but even he could tell that Cairo was bothered by not having a dad. 'Think he lives in Europe somewhere and wears shorts a lot,' added Cairo. 'I saw a photo of him once . . . well it was half a photo – the bottom half. I would recognize his legs . . .' He trailed off and concentrated on shaving away at a long stick – produced

from inside his tracksuit bottoms – with what looked like an industrial potato peeler. Tim's mum usually did all the cooking at home, so he'd never had to use a potato peeler before; he didn't know they could be used on trees! Oh, before you start raiding the kitchen drawers – don't use your parents' potato peeler on a tree; it will snap. Cairo's one is very special.

'Don't you go to school in the village?' Tim asked.

'Nah,' said Cairo, grinning. 'I'm home-taught by my mum. It's quite good really. Today I've been learning about the Three Musketeers.' He pointed at his silly felt-tip-pen moustache.

'Lucky you,' said Tim, wishing he could be home-taught.

'My mum's proper job is running an animal shelter.' The boy waved an arm towards the general direction of the village. 'Hey, why don't you come and see it?'

'Um, erm . . . I'm not really sure,' said Tim hesitantly. He was desperate to make a new friend in the village, if only to have someone to play computer games with or just to kick a football about. However, Cairo did seem a bit odd.

'We've got some really interesting animals.'

Cairo was just as keen to make new friends. Being

home-taught made him quite lonely, and Tim seemed nice and normal, not like the rest of the kids in the village. Cairo's mum didn't ever let him swim in the village pond. She was clever.

'I've also got some really good fizzy drinks . . .' Cairo added quickly. 'And I've made you a sword for the journey.'

Cairo handed Tim the piece of branch he had been working on with the potato peeler; it now looked like a beautifully carved samurai katana.

'Wow, that's brilliant,' gasped Tim, swooshing it around his head.

The katana was amazing. But Tim was also a sucker for fizzy drinks, especially as his mum never let him have them, so the prospect of one of those sealed the deal. Maybe Cairo wasn't *that* odd after all.

'It's this way back, won't take us long,' said Cairo with a friendly smile.

So off the pair trotted back to Cairo's, Tim blissfully unaware that Cairo sometimes liked pouring custard into his wellingtons to see what it felt like on his feet. Probably best not to tell Tim though. He might change his mind about going to Cairo's house and then we'd have to stop the book and just hum for a bit.

3
A MAGNIFICENT BEAST

The walk to Cairo's house was a lot longer than Tim expected, but he didn't really mind. He enjoyed listening to his new friend talking about his favourite topics, which were animals, sauces and people called Keith. Cairo was a bit odd, but a good kind of odd. Not the dribbling and barking-at-the-moon kind of odd.

Cairo had just started telling him about a cheese and pickle sandwich he'd found on the top deck of a bus once, when they suddenly arrived at his house. I say 'suddenly' because it just appeared at the end of a winding path, like a giant had thrown it there from another country and this was where it had landed.

The house was a long, light-blue bungalow with a number of sheds and outhouses attached to and scattered around it. On the roof was one of the biggest satellite dishes Tim had ever seen. He thought it must have been able to pick up channels from all over the world.

'It doesn't work, never has,' said Cairo, when he saw Tim looking at the satellite. 'It doesn't even have a wire you can plug it in with.'

'Oh,' said Tim, feeling somewhat disappointed. 'Why don't you take it down then?'

Cairo laughed. 'Because it's the weight of a thousand hippos! It's only good for target practice . . . anyway, come over here – I've got something really good to show you.'

'Is it the fizzy drinks?' Tim's eyes lit up.

'Er . . . not exactly – we'll get to them in a minute, after I've shown you this thing.'

Tim stopped thinking about the fizzy drinks as soon as he saw what Cairo had behind the back of the shed. Standing there was a tall, long-necked, hairy animal with a very proud face.

'This is Ludo,' said Cairo, patting the animal on the side of neck. 'He's a llama. Mum saved him from some farm in Wales.'

Tim approached the snorting llama as slowly and cautiously as he could. Usually he would have just looked at it from a safe distance, but he didn't want Cairo to think he was scared.

Ludo was a magnificent beast, covered in beautiful thick black hair from the bottom of his legs all the way to the top of his head. But as Tim got closer he noticed something sad about the llama's appearance. His long neck kept lolling forward and dragging on the ground; not all upright and straight like the necks of llamas he'd seen in books.

'We think he's unhappy because he's not with the rest of his llama mates,' said Cairo, patting Ludo's neck again. 'He's been on his own for a few weeks now, but luckily Mum is going to collect the rest of them later this week.'

'The rest of them?' asked Tim.

'Yep, there's another ten. They've all been mistreated or something like that.' Cairo's happy-go-lucky attitude flicked to anger for a brief second as he talked. 'They were in a right state when we found them.'

Tim took a steadying breath and reached out to carefully touch Ludo's hairy neck. It was incredibly soft.

'C'mon, don't be scared,' encouraged Cairo from the other side of the animal.

'Don't llamas spit at people?' asked Tim, bravely touching Ludo's neck for a second time.

'Nah, only if you really annoy them. They're quite friendly animals really, much misunderstood.'

This gave Tim the confidence to give Ludo a proper stroke.

'That's it,' said Cairo softly. 'He likes the odd tickle as well.'

Ludo seemed to really appreciate the attention and his head slowly started to lift and move towards Tim.

His intense brown eyes locked on to Tim's.

Tim could sense that the llama was measuring him up. He dared not move an inch as the huge llama looked him up and down. Then, after what seemed like an age, Ludo blinked slowly, gave a teeny tiny nod of approval and resumed casually chewing on some grass, as though nothing had happened. A warm glow covered Tim's body like a thick coat. Meeting Ludo was awesome!

'He likes you!' said Cairo cheerfully. 'You've made some new friends today!'

'I think I have,' replied Tim with a smirk. 'Ludo is probably a bit nicer than you though!'

Cairo chuckled.

A woman in blue overalls appeared by the side of the shed. Her clothes and hands were covered in mud; however, her face and hair were immaculate, as though she'd just left the hairdressers. She had very shiny black hair that touched her shoulders, and warm, friendly smiley eyes. On her feet were a pair of mismatched wellington boots, just like Cairo's.

'This is my mum . . . Molly,' said Cairo proudly. He didn't seem the slightest bit embarrassed. Molly was clearly one of those rare cool mums you occasionally meet.

Tim smiled, and mumbled a 'hi'. This is the standard greeting from an eleven-year-old boy, I'm told.

'I see you've met Ludo then,' she said, smiling at Tim and giving the llama a big pat on his back.

Tim nodded and stroked Ludo on the side of his neck again. 'Yeah, he's really cool.'

'I think so too,' said Molly. 'He's had a rough time recently, but he's getting back to his best. And I'm going to collect the rest of the llamas in the van tomorrow.'

'Are we going to keep them?' asked Cairo.

'We don't have room to keep eleven llamas long term,' said Molly sadly. 'Our field is already turning into a zoo. Plus the goats . . . well, you know they aren't keen on visitors.'

'Oh yes, I forgot about the goats,' said Cairo, rubbing his chin and staring off into the distance.

Tim was totally baffled. Zoos? Goats? What on earth were Cairo and Molly talking about?

'So what we need is to find someone foolish enough to give eleven llamas a nice new home,' said Cairo slowly.

'Yes, yes we do. Now who could that be?' added Molly, looking directly at Tim.

23

It sounds like Cairo and Molly are dropping a massive hint to Tim doesn't it? Well, you're right – they are. However, Tim won't catch up with the rest of us for at least the next three chapters. The nincompoop! Nincompoop was a very rude word when I used to play football.

4

THE WORST FARMER EVER

For the first month in their new farm, the Gravy family watched Frank do absolutely no farming whatsoever. He had spent a lot of time cultivating a big, thick, bushy beard that apparently was an essential piece of equipment for someone new to farming. He'd also looked at a few magazines with tractors in them, but that was about it.

In their second month on the farm, Frank started going outside. Tim would catch him staring blankly at patches of grass or looking at trees with his hands on his hips. This must have been a new version of farming that Tim wasn't aware of. The beard was longer and thicker, and Frank had taken to wearing thick lumberjack shirts and rolling the bottom of his jeans up to his shins. Occasionally he'd sit in the back yard chomping on a long blade of grass and looking off into the distance. Tim was worried his dad might be going mad.

Then, one Saturday, Frank suddenly sprung into life, as if someone had whacked him over the head with a huge book called *Start Farming, Lazy*.

First up were crops, you know, like vegetables and wheat and stuff. Tim had watched his dad and his annoying little sister, Fiona, through the kitchen window as they tried to plant them. Well, Fiona was pointing out where the seeds should be planted. She wasn't actually doing any work. It took Frank ages, and he seemed to get angrier and angrier the longer it went on. Tim was convinced he saw him spend an entire hour arguing with his spade.

The next morning, the whole Gravy family were outside before breakfast, chasing crows away from the seeds. Apart from Fiona of course, who was lounging in a chair with some hot blackcurrant juice and yelling out orders. It was a totally pointless exercise, as every single seed was gobbled up in a matter of minutes.

Frank went and sat quietly in a tree for a few hours after that; Tim was sure he could see his bottom lip quivering. Monica and Beetroot tried to lure him down with some sticky-toffee pudding, but even the prospect of dessert for breakfast couldn't shift him. Fiona ate the sticky-toffee pudding five minutes later and blamed it on the crows.

Then came the chickens. A large crate of ten scruffy brown hens. As Frank hadn't read the chapter on chickens in his farming book yet, he left them in the main field to peck at the ground for the night until he decided what to do with them. Big mistake . . .

Why? Because of leopards . . . I mean *foxes*. Those sneaky foxes are everywhere! Look out of any window after dark and I'm sure you'll see at least seven of them . . . I'm right aren't I?

Those foxes had a right old night in the Gravys' unguarded field. The easiest chicken dinner a fox could ever imagine. They even had time to make roast potatoes. The chickens didn't stand a chance. However, I did hear a rumour that one called Cecil got away. Cecil is a big name in the chicken community.

Frank went and sat in the tree all night after he lost the chickens. Tim lay in bed worrying about him. He was used to seeing his dad return home from work every evening in a suit and then just sit around watching telly with the rest of the family. At weekends he would usually play cards, take them swimming and sometimes have a go on a computer game, which he was rubbish at. Now all he did was fiddle about with the farm. He had no time for Tim,

Monica or even Fiona. He didn't even arm-wrestle with Beetroot anymore, and that was their favourite thing ever. Well, it was Beetroot's . . . she always won.

What Frank did have was loads of splinters in his bottom from sitting in trees. However, as he was trying to tweezer them out, he had an idea. A brilliant idea . . . sort of.

5
A PIG CALLED TREVOR

The very next day Frank drove somewhere and returned two hours later with a huge pig sitting in the back seat. It was already covered in muck, and had spread a lot more over the inside of the car.

Frank climbed out of the car holding his nose and pulling one of those faces people pull when their nostrils have been filled up with a horrific stench.

'Have you done something in the car?' he said to the pig through the window.

The pig looked at him briefly and let out a squeal of delight. Truth be told, he hadn't done anything in the car; he was just an incredibly happy pig. Imagine how happy you'd be if you won the lottery, every single race at sports day and nailed the top score on a computer game, all in the same afternoon. Well, that's how happy this pig was. So it was slightly odd that he was called Evil Trevor by his former owners.

He wasn't evil at all, but he was called Trevor.

With one hand clamped firmly over his nose and mouth, Frank opened the car door and let Trevor hop out, which he did with much glee. The pig snorted around the driveway for a few minutes and poked his nose in a few nooks and crannies before rolling on his back a few times. He finished this little song and dance by bowing his head towards Frank as though he wanted to be politely stroked. Frank slowly, but cautiously, patted Trevor on the head, and he let out another squeal of delight. Trevor, not Frank. It would be odd if Frank had squealed. Trevor then ran around in a circle a few times, and did a little piggy jig.

Trevor got even more excited when the three Gravy children appeared outside, letting out happy squeals of their own and jigging about as they approached him. Within seconds, they were all hugging, patting and tickling him.

Then the back door flew open and Beetroot stormed through it. She was wearing a dressing gown and her hair was soaking wet. Obviously the piggish commotion outside had forced her out of her shower or bath. I'm not sure which as I've never visited the Gravys' bathroom so I don't know what they have – probably both; most people do nowadays. In my day, once a week, my father threw buckets of cold water at us while we stood in our undercrackers in the garden. Now that's a wash.

'No. No. No. No! NO!' screamed Beetroot from the side of the house.

'It's just a—' began Frank, before he was interrupted.

'No. No. No. NO. NO! NO! NO!' repeated Beetroot. She was going really purple now.

'Why can't we keep the piggy, Mummy?' pleaded Fiona.

'No. No. NO. NO. NO! NO! NO!' screamed Beetroot, this time with an added pointing finger, which we all know means 'take it back' in angry mum language.

'Je n'aime pas . . . le jambon,' she whispered to Frank, through gritted teeth.

Beetroot always tried to talk French to Frank when she didn't want the children to find out what she was saying. The only problem was Frank was rubbish at French. He just shrugged at her.

Monica, who was doing French in her exams, did understand the point her mum was trying to get across. She gave Trevor a friendly cheerio pat on the head and ushered him towards the car. Tim and Fiona looked on sadly. But probably not as sadly as they would have looked if Trevor had appeared in a bacon sandwich six months later.

Frank sighed deeply and opened the car door. Another farming failure to add to the list. Even Trevor seemed to sense that living on a working farm probably wouldn't end well, and hopped back into the vehicle.

As the car drove away Trevor's piggy face appeared in the back window. He looked sad for the first time ever in his short life, then let out a huge squeal of delight. This time he *had* pooped in the car and he was mighty happy with himself.

Frank, understandably, wasn't.

So what did happen to Trevor in the end? Rumour has it he is releasing a new hip-hop album next year. Whatever hip-hop is.

6
THE GRIM PHONE CALL

A few days later, Tim was trying to finish up some very boring homework about why mice like cheese. All he'd written in answer to the question was:

Because thye do.

He was yet to spot he'd spelled the word 'they' wrong when the phone rang. His bedroom was directly above where the landline lived, so he could sometimes hear parts of the conversation. This sounded like a really bad one. He could hear the muffled sound of his dad doing a lot of apologizing.

Tim crept out of his room and ducked down at the top of the stairs so he could hear the call a little more clearly.

'I know, I know, it's been a tough few months settling in,' said Frank in a serious voice.

There was a pause while he listened to what the

person said at the other end of the line.

'Well, yes, I'm trying to make money, but I've had a few hiccups. It's a very different style of living out here in the countryside. Harder than I thought, to be honest.'

He paused again.

'I totally understand, and I can only apologize again for the situation. I will try to rectify it as soon as possible and pay back some of the money that I've borrowed.'

Another pause.

'Yes, I understand I am in danger of losing the farm. I'm very aware it's important.'

Tim noticed his dad scrunch his eyes up tightly and start rubbing his forehead as he listened to the person at the other end of the phone. He looked really upset and worried. Tim had never seen his dad look like this before; he didn't like it at all.

'OK, I understand, and thanks again for the call,' said Frank before he put the phone down.

He puffed out his cheeks and muttered something under his breath, then walked dejectedly back into the lounge, closing the door behind him.

Tim tiptoed down the stairs as softly as he could and positioned himself by the handle of the door. He knew his dad would be telling his mum about the phone call.

The lounge door was made of thick oak and it was really hard to make out what they were saying. He heard the words 'debt', 'bank', 'repossess', 'big trouble' and 'Scotland', before Monica tapped him on the shoulder, making him jump out of his skin.

'What you doing, nosy?' she asked. She had some kind of bright green beauty gloop splattered all over her face, which made Tim do a double jump of terror.

'Sssh will you,' he whispered urgently once he had recovered. 'I think something bad is happening with the farm. They're talking about it.'

'What do you mean something bad about the farm?'

Tim could just about make out Monica's eyebrows forming a sticky green frown.

'What does *repossess* mean?' he asked.

Monica's mouth dropped open, and some of the face mask plopped on to the floor. 'It's not good,' she replied. The handle of the door turned. Monica and Tim looked at each other and within a split second they had both scampered back to their rooms.

It was another night of worry for Tim. He was trying to work out what it all meant. Was the house being taken away? Did they have no money? Would they have to sell their beds and his games console? Would they be moving up to Scotland? Did that mean living with his weird auntie?

Moving in with his Scottish auntie would probably be the worst thing ever. She wasn't actually Scottish. She just lived there in a horrible, small, stinky, cat-filled terraced house in one of the big cities.

Cat litter trays filled every room of her house and they only seemed to get emptied once a month. The cats wouldn't let visitors sit on any of the sofas or seats, so most conversations were held standing up in the kitchen, with the door shut, while an army of cats lurked on the other side, hissing and scratching. Inside the kitchen wasn't much better, to be honest. Huge stinky bowls of cat food were perched on nearly every surface and across the floor. All the cats were called Florence, which was either very confusing or brilliant; I can't work out which.

Tim's brain churned these thoughts over and over for ages. He didn't want to move to Scotland, so he needed to help his dad get the farm making some money. But how? Then, in a flash of inspiration . . . he finally had the idea that Cairo and Molly had been so clearly hinting at a few chapters ago.

7
THE DEAL

When Tim came downstairs in the morning, he saw his dad sitting at the kitchen table stirring his tea round and round and round and round. This was odd as he didn't take sugar – what a waste of a spoon!

Frank had huge dark circles under his eyes, and his hair and beard were all over the place, not neat and tidy like usual. He was also wearing Beetroot's yellow dressing gown, which was far too small for him.

'You OK, Dad?' asked Tim.

'What . . . oh yes, I'm fine . . . I'm fine . . . totally fine.' Frank continued to stir his now stone-cold tea, looking into its dark brown swirls.

Tim thought about his next sentence for a long time before he said it. He was trying to judge if this was the right time, as Frank looked very sad. Maybe this would help to cheer him up?

'I was thinking, Dad . . . the seeds, chickens and the pig didn't work out, but I've got a new friend who might be able to give us something that could make money for the farm,' he said quickly.

'That's nice,' replied Frank, who was clearly not listening. He continued looking blankly into his cold tea.

'My friend's mum, Molly, runs an animal shelter, and they've got a llama,' continued Tim. 'It's got really soft wool that we could farm.'

Frank remained silent for a few minutes and then looked up. He wasn't smiling as Tim had hoped. 'I don't think one llama is enough for a decent wool farm, Tim. You'd need loads of llamas to produce enough wool for farming, and besides, I don't know the first thing about llama farming. It's not like doing sheep or cows.'

'You didn't know anything about chickens or pigs, but you were willing to give them a try,' said Tim, feeling a little hurt that Frank wasn't taking his idea seriously.

'That's true,' admitted Frank.

'Well, why not try a llama? My friend is getting another ten soon, so we'd have more than enough. We could have them for free and they probably wouldn't cost much to keep.' Tim was just guessing now.

Frank finally stopped stirring the cup of cold tea. The word 'free' was one of his favourites. The lines on his forehead deepened. Tim knew this was a sign he was really thinking. He did this every time Tim persuaded him to buy a new computer game, especially if Tim had come up with a really good reason as to why they definitely needed that particular game.

Frank got up without saying anything and wandered out of the kitchen. Tim could hear him walking around the house, muttering to himself, opening doors and then shutting them again. This was also part of his thinking process. A few minutes later he reappeared in the kitchen, the frown lines had gone and his eyes seemed a little brighter.

'OK, I've thought it over . . . and . . . I'm willing to

give it a whirl,' he said. 'On two conditions.'

'Name them,' said Tim excitedly.

'First, if they spit at me they can go back straight away.'

'They rarely spit, Dad. In fact, they are a much misunderstood animal,' said Tim, quoting Cairo.

'Second, you will be in charge of clearing up all their mess. We can sell it for manure.'

Tim was less sure about this one. But it was worth it if it meant they could have Ludo and his friends living in their field.

'You have yourself a deal.' A smile broke out on Tim's face; he couldn't hide the delight that was surging through his body. 'This is going to be brilliant!'

'It better be,' muttered Frank under his breath, his face dropping back into serious mode again. 'Or we won't be living here much longer.'

8
THE HERD ARRIVES

Cairo was waving at Tim like a nutter through the window of the large animal transporter as Molly parked it up at the Gravys' farm. Tim waved casually back. He was bursting with excitement inside, but wanted to appear as cool as possible about the prospect of eleven llamas living in their spare field. He was a proper farmer's son now.

Tim had noticed that his dad was slightly less excited. During the last few days, Frank had started scribbling loads of numbers and sums in a little black notepad that he carried around in his back trouser pocket. He was always checking it and looking worried. Tim didn't like the little black notepad – it made Frank really unhappy.

Cairo expertly unloaded all the llamas from the transporter and led them into the spare field, which was across the road from the main farmhouse. Frank had started building a disastrous attempt at a princess castle in a corner of the main field, under the orders of Fiona, and it was no place for llamas.

The spare field wasn't the greatest – as people seemed to use it as a bit of a dumping ground for rubbish they didn't want – but it had loads of grass and juicy weeds in it for the llamas to munch on.

Frank went and introduced himself to Molly, while Tim and Cairo watched the llamas start slowly exploring their new surroundings. One had teeth that jutted out at the bottom of his mouth, one was very tall, while another had a black flash across his face. At the back was a much happier-looking Ludo. He instantly recognized Tim and strode proudly over for a friendly stroke. Tim patted the llama's neck and rubbed the side of his face while Ludo casually nodded his approval.

'They'll be happy here,' said Cairo, with a beaming grin. 'They had a really rough time at their last place. Really nasty.' His smile dropped away.

Tim noticed the already familiar flash of anger cross Cairo's face when he talked about animal cruelty. He was impressed by how much his friend really cared about animals.

'Eventually their hair will grow back and the scars

43

will heal,' Cairo added, his face softening. 'Then you can think about what you and your dad are going to do with them.'

'I know what *I'll* be doing,' said Tim with a sigh. 'Shovelling manure. I promised my dad that's what I'd do if we got them.'

Cairo laughed. Tim didn't.

'I'll get you a massive spade for your birthday, maybe one of those snow shovel things,' said Cairo.

Ludo had now left Tim's side and had walked purposefully to the main gate into the field. He stood there tall and firm, looking out down the road.

'What's he doing?' asked Tim, slightly hurt that his favourite llama had just wandered off.

'Hmmm, interesting . . .' muttered Cairo. 'I think he might be a guard llama. Some of them are like that – farmers use them like security guards to protect their livestock. Odd, isn't it?'

'So he's just going to stand there as a lookout?'

'It certainly looks like it. He's the boss; that's his job.'

Frank came over to Tim and Cairo. He was furiously scribbling in his notepad, his face a creased ball of concentration. 'Molly tells me we are going to have to get a big shed for the llamas to live in,' he said, without looking up from his book.

'You'll also need a water trough, regular fresh hay, feed and obviously . . . a manure shovel,' added Cairo, with a wink at Tim.

Frank gritted his teeth, turned a page in his notepad and began scribbling again.

'We've saved them from some very cruel treatment, Dad. This will be paradise compared to that horrible place they were in.'

Frank ignored Tim, stopped writing and tucked his pencil behind his ear.

'When do you think the wool will be ready?' He directed his question straight at Cairo, as though he was an expert on farming llamas.

Luckily for Frank, Cairo's llama knowledge was pretty good, as he'd some read books about them, unlike yours truly. As a professional footballer, I didn't have time for reading books . . . I only learned how to spell llama three weeks ago!

'It's going to be a while I reckon,' replied Cairo. 'However, some good food, shelter and friendly owners, and they'll be fine after Christmas.'

Frank's face dropped; this wasn't the news he wanted to hear, Christmas was months away. It was going to cost him loads just to feed and shelter the llamas before

he could make any money out of their wool.

'Of course you can sell the poo straight away,' said Cairo, pointing at a huge pile of neat brown pellets, like coffee beans, that had just landed by Frank's feet.

Tim screwed up his eyes and felt all squirmy inside. He really didn't want to be clearing up llama poo on his first day as a llama farmer. Suddenly his left leg became very warm. Tim looked down. An arc of llama wee was spraying on to his jeans.

Next to him stood a grey llama with a huge grin on his face. Maybe this wasn't such a good idea after all, thought Tim.

9

THE KICK-ABOUT

When he wasn't shovelling llama poo, which actually wasn't that bad with a huge snow shovel, Tim found out that Cairo had never properly played football. So he was keen to show his new friend why it was the greatest sport ever and to make him understand the ecstatic thrill of scoring a goal. Cairo didn't seem to be bothered by these bold claims. He thought snail racing was the greatest sport ever . . . even if it did take three weeks to finish a race.

Tim regretted showing Cairo how to play football almost immediately. He had never met *anyone* as bad as Cairo. He might have been brilliant at looking after animals, but he was shocking with a ball at his feet.

Cairo's main problem was that he had no control over the power of his kicks. He just blasted everything from anywhere. Everything was a shot for Cairo. If he was really lucky, he'd get one on target and it would fly past Tim and into the imaginary net. But most of the time the ball would soar high and wide – crashing against the side of the house, the fence, a window or anything that happened to be in the yard or passing by it. Even Fiona was in the firing line. One misplaced volley barely clipped her little finger, but she fell to the ground as if she'd been shot by a sniper.

'YEEEOOOOOOOWWWWWWLLLLLL! MY BEAUTIFUL FACE!' she howled at the top of her voice.

Tim and Cairo ran over to her straight away.

'Calm down, will you?' begged Tim, hoping Beetroot wouldn't hear. 'It didn't go anywhere near your face.'

'My beautiful face,' Fiona sobbed again. Both hands were now clamped firmly across her nose, stemming an imaginary stream of blood. 'My modelling career is ruined! My eye could have fallen out.' She let out another piercing scream for good measure.

'It didn't go anywhere near your face, Fiona,' repeated Tim through gritted teeth. 'Now stop screaming.'

'YEEEEOOOOOOWWWWWWWW!' Fiona let out an even louder and bigger scream.

The kitchen door flew open and Beetroot came running out. She scooped up Fiona and gave her one of the biggest cuddles a mum could give.

'My . . . my . . . my . . . f-f-face, Mummy,' wailed Fiona. 'T-T-Tim kicked the ball into my face, from an inch away.'

'I did not!' shouted Tim. 'It just brushed her finger.'

This made Fiona scream even louder. Beetroot nodded sympathetically at Tim, but she didn't want to get into an argument into who did what; it was never worth it.

'Let's see if we can find something inside to make it better,' said Beetroot soothingly to Fiona, calmly stroking her long hair.

'Sweets?' asked Fiona, her tears and sobbing stopping almost instantly.

'Maybe,' replied Beetroot. They went back inside the farmhouse and Tim kicked the ground in frustration.

'I think we've lost the ball,' said Cairo, adding insult to injury.

'Where did it go?' Tim huffed.

'Bounced out across the road.'

'Probably went in the field opposite; we'll get it later. I've got a bag of spares.'

They played for another five minutes or so before Cairo belted another huge shot wide of the goal and out across the road. Tim shook his head and flapped his hands in a 'we'll get it later' gesture and picked another ball out the bag. That one didn't last long either.

Tim gritted his teeth and tried to muster up a fake smile to show that he wasn't annoyed – even though he was inwardly fuming that his new friend had managed to lose three balls in less than ten minutes. In the city he would have gone and played with someone else, but in the country he only had Cairo to play with, and he didn't want to lose his only friend over a simple kick-about.

'Sorry,' called Cairo. He looked embarrassed. 'I'm not very good, am I?'

'I think you're getting better,' said Tim, trying to be encouraging, 'But no, at this moment you aren't the greatest. I've only got this ball left, but at least it will be easy to find if we lose it.'

Tim held up a neon orange ball and bounced it on the yard towards Cairo, who immediately swung his left leg at it and lobbed it back over Tim's head and out across the road into the field opposite.

'Ooops, sorreeee!'

Tim sighed. 'Let's go and get them.'

Tim and Cairo looked everywhere for the footballs but couldn't find them. They weren't on the road, in any bushes or up any trees. They scanned the field full of llamas but there was nothing there either. Ludo was by the gate as usual. A few llamas were standing in one corner and a few were sitting down, but there were no balls to be seen. Even the neon orange ball had seemingly disappeared.

'Have you seen our footballs, Ludo?' asked Tim, giving the tall black llama a stroke.

The llama stared back at him and then looked away.

'I didn't kick them that hard,' said Cairo, scratching the top of his head thoughtfully. 'They can't all have gone missing.'

'Perhaps someone pinched them all?' replied Tim.

'Maybe, but I haven't seen anyone go down the road.'

'Do llamas eat footballs?' asked Tim, as he noticed a white llama with a black flash across his nose chewing furiously on something pink. Possibly part of the discarded sofa.

'They eat grass, Tim,' replied Cairo with a chuckle. He followed Tim's gaze. 'Well . . . mostly. I doubt they'd have much interest in plastic balls.'

They returned to the farmhouse and found Fiona sitting on the step waiting for them, sucking on the biggest lolly ever. She looked very pleased with herself.

'I got the biggest lolly ever, because you injured me,' she said smugly.

Tim tried to ignore her but he wanted one of those lollies as well. This was turning into a bad day. Where had all his footballs gone? Had Fiona pinched them? Had someone from the village stolen them? Had they all exploded with the force of Cairo's terrible shots? It was a big mystery.

10
THE WAITING GAME

On the way to school the following day, Tim found one of the missing balls sitting in the middle of the yard. It was totally flat – as though someone had been playing with it so much that all the air had come out of it. He held the ball up to his face and sniffed it. I've no idea why he sniffed the ball. It offered him no clue as to where it had been whatsoever. It smelt of plastic and grass, like every other football does.

Tim looked out of the farm and up and down the road. There was no one about. He could see nothing but Ludo standing motionless by the gate in the field opposite, like he did every day. Tim paced around looking for unusual footprints in the compacted dirt. This was also a fruitless task, as all he ended up doing was getting confused by the footprints he was leaving himself.

The next day, before school, there was another

flat football waiting for Tim in the yard. Once again a sniff revealed nothing. 'Ha, ha, ha!' he shouted into the air, to no one in particular. 'Very, *very* funny. Good prank guys! You can come out now.'

He waited silently. Nobody appeared. This was very frustrating. Tim sniffed the ball again. He should really stop doing that now, don't you think?

That night, Tim asked his dad if he knew anything about the missing footballs.

'Nope,' replied Frank, in a completely unhelpful manner. 'I've been trying to work out when the wool on these llamas is going to get good enough to sell. Your manure bags aren't making much. Plus, I've got Fiona's princess castle to build. So I haven't really got time for your footballs.'

'But . . . can you get me some new ones?'

Frank did a small intake of breath, which was always a bad sign. 'We've not really got the spare

54

cash to be buying footballs,' he replied. 'However, if we can sell the llama wool, then I'll see what we can do.'

'But that will be ages away,' moaned Tim, flapping his arms around in a sulky manner.

'I know,' muttered Frank, getting out his little black notepad. Oh how Tim hated that little notepad. Every time Frank opened it he got more down in the dumps.

(Interestingly, the notepad didn't want to be the cause of Frank's sadness either. It'd always wanted to be something a three-year-old scribbled in and then lost down the back of the sofa. But then notepads have different ambitions to humans.)

'I'm sorry, Tim,' said Frank after a long pause. He sighed heavily. 'That's just the way things are, I'm afraid. You'll have to be patient.'

Tim gritted his teeth and tried to suppress his frustration. 'You'll have to be patient' was one of his least favourite phrases. It never meant anything good.

The next day was a Saturday, so Tim decided he was going to stay up all night and find out once and for all what was going on with his disappearing/reappearing footballs. He got an essential survival kit together: a

sleeping bag, two cartons of juice, some crisps and two Lego figures – and set up camp on the low sloped roof of the toolshed that overlooked the farmyard.

As it got dark, Tim realized he'd forgotten to bring a torch and so couldn't see anything, apart from large, dark scary shapes; and as I'm sure you already know, the more you look at stuff in the dark, the scarier it becomes. To make things even worse, even though Tim couldn't *see* anything, he could *hear* plenty, and after a while everything was starting to make him jump with fear. A rustle in the undergrowth, the hoot of an owl, a cough from inside the house, the wind through the trees, car wheels on gravel, a chirrup, a snuffle, a light whistle. Everything sounded like it was coming to get him. He pulled the sleeping bag over his head and tried to block out the sounds, but it wasn't helping.

One sound that didn't seem to stop was a distinctly familiar *tap, tap, tap, thwack* noise. It was quite muffled, but it was definitely coming from somewhere not too far from the shed roof. Tim strained his ears and bravely tried to peer out into the darkness. *Tap, tap, tap, thwack*. There it was again!

Tim settled back into his sleeping bag and mulled over what it could be. A bird pecking at some wood?

A squirrel cracking a nut? Fiona trying to break into a sweet shop?

That was all he could come up with before he fell asleep.

11
THE DISCOVERY

'TIM . . . TIM . . . TIM!'

Tim slowly peeled the sleeping bag away from the side of his face. He had no idea what time it was, but it must have been fairly early in the morning. There was a low thick fog around the house and the farm that made it hard to see more than ten steps in front of the shed roof he was perched on.

'TIM! TIM! TIM!' came the voice again, but this time with more urgency. 'COME AND LOOK AT THIS . . . *TIM!*'

Tim peered down the road as a small figure emerged from the fog waving his arms frantically over his head. It was Cairo. Tim had forgotten they had arranged to meet at a stupidly early time in the morning.

'Get down off that roof and come and see this . . . you won't believe it. I'm not sure if I believe it!'

Tim wriggled out of his sleeping bag and slid off the top of the shed roof with all the grace of a bowl of soup trying to enter a dance competition. He quickly followed Cairo, who was waving him towards the llama field. What he saw next was one of the most amazing things he had ever seen in his life; even better than the lawnmower museum he'd visited last summer.

The llamas were playing football!

It was totally A-MAY-ZING. The llamas were pinging a series of short, fast passes to each other; smashing thunderous shots back off the fence and dribbling the ball as though someone had smeared it in glue and stuck it to their feet.

Tim's eyes bulged out of his head when he saw what was going on in the field. He made a series of 'eh', 'wha' and 'do-ya' sounds before he eventually managed to form a real sentence, although it wasn't a very good one.

'The llamas are playing football!' he blurted out.

'We are not dreaming,' replied Cairo. 'I've already pinched myself a thousand times. Shall I pinch you just to double check?'

'The llamas are playing football!' repeated the stunned Tim.

'Yes, yes they are,' Cairo agreed.

'The llamas are playing football!'

'Don't say it again,' warned Cairo, 'or I really will pinch you.'

'They are llamas . . .' Tim said slowly, 'and they AARRRRRRGGGHHHHH!' He jumped back, grabbing his arm.

'I did warn you!' said Cairo apologetically. 'Anyway, at least we both know we're awake now.'

Tim was captivated by the scene unfolding in front of him. The llamas had all the basic skills; heading, shooting, tackling and passing. A few of them could juggle the ball on one foot, some could do headed keepie-ups, and Tim was convinced he saw one of them try a rainbow flick. There are professional footballers being paid a bazillion pounds a week that can't even kick a ball with their left foot, let alone successfully pull off a rainbow flick. It was truly a sight to behold. For the record, I was equally brilliant with both feet.

The only llama that wasn't playing football was Ludo. He remained by the gate, looking out into the road. He didn't seem to be bothered in the slightest about his llama friends playing the beautiful game; it was as if he had better things to do. What these things were, I've no idea. Perhaps he was thinking

about corned beef. Corned beef was a big deal in my day. Mmmm . . . corned beef.

Tim simply *had* to tell everyone he had the best football-playing llamas in the country, maybe even the best football-playing animals in the whole world. Lucky for Tim, the rest of the world believes everything they are told by eleven-year-old boys, don't they?

They don't?!

Well in that case, we might have a rough ride ahead.

12
THE SECRET

Tim and Cairo watched the llamas play football for hours. The fog had cleared and the llamas didn't seem to be at all bothered by their new spectators, even with Cairo occasionally hooting 'Olé, olé!' after some sublime passing, or singing 'Score in a minute! We're gonna score in a minute!' at every crashing shot. Cairo had never been to a real football match before. He had just heard that this was the kind of thing football fans did sometimes.

'They've obviously got more confident now they've started playing in the day, rather than just at night,' said Cairo, after cheering a particularly spectacular volley by a completely white llama with a light grey flash across his nose and horrendous sticky-out teeth.

'Yes,' said Tim, still trying to come to terms with the amazing sight in front of him. 'But why are they are so good at football?'

'Perhaps they were like this when we got them,' replied Cairo, mid-clap at a fantastic forty-yard-long ball.

'Maybe, but they were in an absolute state before, they were so weak. I think something must have happened to them in this field.'

'A passing wizard?' suggested Cairo.

'Ha, ha,' replied Tim shrugging off his friend's unhelpful comment. 'Hang on . . . their ball has got stuck in the corner of the field; we'd better go and get it.'

The duo wandered over to far side of the field to look for the ball. This meant having to rifle through all the junk that had been dumped over the years.

A rusty hovercraft, a metal trunk filled with wooden shavings, a mouldy jockey's outfit, a cricket bat with a broken handle, a lime-green sink, a vacuum cleaner with a hole in the top, a clock with no hands, a pink sofa with no cushions, the junk went on and on. Eventually Tim found the ball wedged among a stack of old chimneys and leaned in to fish it out.

'Hey, hey, look at me in my new hat,' said Cairo, jumping up and down on the pink sofa.

Tim looked up and saw Cairo doing an odd little dance with a large black thing on his head. He was wobbling it from side to side as he approached Tim, singing as he went. 'Oohh look at me in my new posh hat, I'm off to the sixth-form prom tonight, off to the sixth-form prommmmmmmm tonnnniiiiggghhhtttt!'

'That's not a hat, Cairo; it's one of those things witches have . . . what are they called?'

'A cauldron,' exclaimed Cairo, his eyes lighting up. 'Maybe some witches gave the llamas a potion and that made them great at football?'

'Give it here,' said Tim, grabbing it from Cairo's head. He examined it thoroughly from top to bottom. 'I think it might be an urn . . . you know, what they put dead people in instead of putting them in the ground.'

'URRRRRR! I had it on my head!' screamed Cairo, frantically brushing his hair.

'It says Arthur Muckluck on it,' said Tim, rubbing some mud off the side of the urn.

'Who's Arthur Muckluck?' wondered Cairo out loud.

'I think I've heard the name before,' Tim said thoughtfully. 'My grandad talked about him. A famous singer or something . . . lemme have a think.'

'We don't have to think nowadays, we can just check on my phone,' said Cairo, pulling a battered silver phone from his pocket.

'That phone is older than me!' exclaimed Tim. 'Are you sure it has the internet?'

Cairo ignored Tim's slap down, tapped my name into his phone and waited for it to do its magic. 'Here we go,' he said eventually, as Tim got as close as possible to see what was on the screen.

Cairo began to read in his poshest voice: '*Ahem, ahem*. Arthur Muckluck was one of the world's greatest footballers. Over fifty England caps, three Cup winners' medals, two Division One league titles and a World Cup win.

'A creative genius, rocket quick, brilliant in the air, composed in front of goal and never scared to make

65

crucial, crunching tackles. He even went in goal on two separate occasions – saved two penalties and kept two clean sheets.'

I'm very happy Cairo's phone has that information on it. It's exactly how I described myself at the start of the book. See, I told you I was the world's greatest footballer ever.

Tim and Cairo looked at each other – their mouths wide open with a mixture of surprise and excitement.

'The llamas must have eaten the ashes of this Arthur Muckluck bloke that were mixed up in all the grass,' said Tim.

'And it's made them all brilliant footballers,' added Cairo.

'Whoa, that is awesome!' they both exclaimed at the same time.

Cairo's eyes widened; a stupid idea had fallen into his brain and knocked the 'eyes wide switch' by mistake. 'I'm going to have a go at the grass, it might make me a better footballer.'

'Be my guest,' replied Tim, stepping back and waving his hand dramatically at the ground as though he spent all afternoon making it.

Cairo bent down, opened his mouth as wide as possible and took a huge bite out of the muddy grass. Tim burst out laughing.

Cairo stood up and began chewing on the lump of turf he had in his mouth. His face said it all. It started with disgust and revulsion, which was quickly replaced by horror when he bit into something that felt like a worm, then a smidgeon of curiosity, before he finally turned green and spat the grass on to the field.

'Nice then?' asked Tim, as Cairo rubbed the inside of his mouth with his fingers.

'*Spppt . . . sppptt . . . spptt!* It was disgusting,' moaned Cairo. 'But if it makes me brilliant at football then it was worth every chew.'

'Let's try it,' said Tim, bouncing the ball towards Cairo.

Cairo miscontrolled his first touch with his knee, swung his right leg, missed the ball completely and fell over in a heap.

'Hmmm, the grass doesn't seem to be working. Perhaps you should eat a load more?' suggested Tim with a grin.

Cairo tried a keepie-up. He managed just one before the ball squirted off to the left. He sighed. 'I think one mouthful is enough for me,' he replied. 'Let's just leave it to the llamas shall we. Besides,

I've decided grass is a little bland for my adventurous taste buds.'

Tim and Cairo weren't to know that the llamas had eaten up all my ashes, so there were none left in the field. I'm clearly very tasty. However, I'm not sure chomping up the power of a brilliant dead footballer actually works on humans. Let me just check . . . nope, it only works on animals, and possibly birds. Definitely not fish though. They can't breathe in fields.

'We can't tell anyone about this,' said Tim, staring down at the urn.

'What? We can't tell anyone about the llamas? But it's the most amazing thing ever! It might even help the farm get some extra money,' cried Cairo.

'No, I don't mean about the llamas; I mean the dead-footballer bit!'

'Oh!' said Cairo with an expert nod. 'I see. Why not?'

'Because everyone will be at it! There'll be dead footballers ground up and scattered everywhere.'

'Zombie footballers . . . cooolllllllll. I'd definitely watch that.'

'No, not zombie footballers. You know what I mean. If anyone asks, we just say we found the llamas like this, and we didn't find this urn. In fact, we should bury the urn deep in the ground and put the pink sofa over it, so nobody finds it.'

A frown formed on Cairo's face. 'But I'm not sure anyone will believe us.'

'What, that we just found them like this?'

'Yes, someone is bound to ask questions,' Cairo said, rubbing his chin thoughtfully.

'What do we say then?'

Cairo lay down in the field and looked up into the sky, closed his eyes and breathed in several deep lungfuls of the air. This must be Cairo's thinking process, thought Tim. He needed to get a new style of thinking like this – tapping a pencil on his teeth just wasn't working for him.

'How about we say we got hold of a herd of rare llamas from high in the Andes,' said Cairo with his eyes still closed.

'The Andes?' said Tim.

'They're big mountains in South America. There are lots of llamas there. But our ones are going to be extra rare.'

'So rare that they are a myth . . . like Bigfoot, or the Yeti,' added Tim gleefully, grasping on to Cairo's idea.

'Exactly,' agreed Cairo. 'Or the three-nosed man of Croydon.'

'*What?*'

'The three-nosed man of Croydon,' Cairo repeated. 'No one has ever seen him, but sometimes the people of Croydon hear these huge mega sneezes. Like tiny earthquakes. Only a man with three noses could do those.'

Tim shook his head in awe. There wasn't a place called Croydon, was there? It sounded like a magical land.

'So we'll just stick with saying they're super-rare llamas, right?' he said out loud.

'Yep,' replied Cairo, opening his eyes. 'And no one will ever find out exactly where the llamas came from – cos the Andes are massive.'

He paused and closed his eyes, as though he was imagining something really cool. 'One more thing,' he said dreamily. 'If there are going to be zombie footballers, can I have my own team?'

13
DINNER AT THE GRAVYS

In most good films I've seen, even the ones with the subtitles, when a boy tells people about the amazing and unbelievable thing he has just seen, no adult will believe him. He'll then spend most of the rest of the story trying to *show* people the brilliant thing he has seen *before* they believe him.

Well, this isn't a very good story, so we do things a little differently around here.

Tim and Cairo told the whole Gravy family, who all immediately rushed out to the field and watched the llamas kicking the ball around for another hour or so. Even Fiona came, and she didn't like football. She had the attention span of an ice cream in an oven.

The llamas seemed to be becoming really confident the more they played, and looked like they were enjoying themselves with their heads held high. Two grey llamas were playing head tennis with each other, while a smaller, sandy-coloured pair were pinging crossfield forty-yard volleys with alarming, pinpoint accuracy. Although best of them all was the llama with the horrendously sticky-out teeth: his feet were a blur as danced and tricked his way round three other llamas before smashing the ball against the pink sofa.

Tim started to feel an overwhelming sense of pride at what he had helped achieve, even though all he'd done was put them in the field.

'That black one hasn't moved yet,' said Fiona.

'Yeah, that's Ludo. He just sort of stands there, watching, like he's the boss or guard of all of them,' replied Tim.

'Perhaps he doesn't like football,' said Fiona. 'I like him the best now; football is rubbish.'

'This is amazing, Tim,' said Beetroot, her eyes shining. 'I can't quite believe what I'm watching.'

'It's brilliant,' added Frank, smiling at him. 'It really is brilliant. How is this happening?'

'They are a very rare breed of llama, from high up in the Andes,' said Tim confidently, trying his hardest to keep a straight face.

'That's quite amazing,' said Frank with a slow nod of his head. 'I've never heard of this kind of llama before.'

'Oh they are very, *very* rare,' added Cairo. 'Only a handful of people in the Andes know about them.'

'Well you are the llama expert, Cairo,' said Frank.

Cairo shot Tim a cheeky wink. The lie had passed its test.

At the dinner table that evening the conversation was happy and full of laughter and chatter about the fantastic llamas. It was also probably the first time they had ever all sat down and talked about the 'beautiful game' together for longer than two seconds.

'I reckon you could make some money out of the llamas' football skills,' said Cairo, through a mouthful of roast chicken and mash. His table manners were really rather shocking.

'That's right, we could,' added Tim eagerly. 'Get people to pay to watch them play . . . or, better still, get them to play against a team of humans and sell tickets to the match!'

'Don't be silly,' said Frank gently. 'They might be great at football, but they're still just llamas; they don't know anything about tactics or positions or how the game even works.'

'We could train them,' said Tim, refusing to be beaten down. 'They can pass, shoot, dribble, head, take dead balls and have some pretty cheeky tricks up their sleeves. Better than some real players.'

Frank rubbed his beard. Making money out of llama poo and some wool after Christmas wasn't going to keep the farm running forever. Since taking on the llamas, he had spent the rest of his time building Fiona's princess castle and reading books on beekeeping, but he wasn't getting far with either of them. Perhaps this wasn't the stupidest idea; it wasn't every day he saw a load of llamas being brilliant at football. However, like every proper dad he had to ask questions first. In the *Secret Rule Book of Being a Father* it clearly states that you are never allowed to agree with *anything* your children say straight away. Oops! I've told you about the *Secret Rule Book of Being a Father* . . . ignore what I just said.

'But who would train them?' asked Frank. 'It's going to take some time, and I don't know enough about football to do it.'

'I could do it,' said Tim excitedly. 'I know loads about football.'

'I could do it,' shouted Fiona, banging her knife and fork on the table. 'I will do it for payment in sweets. Large sweets . . . bigger than my head!'

Frank chuckled at both of them. 'It would be great if you could train them, but you've both got school. Proper footballers have to train every single day.'

'That's not true,' replied Tim, pushing his plate away. 'They get loads of time off and only train in the mornings.'

'Well, that still doesn't give you enough time to train them full-time and do school.'

'I could be the assistant manager, Dad,' said Tim,

determined not to give up. 'Perhaps I could get a real football manager to help out. There are loads of managers out there with no jobs.'

Frank laughed. 'I don't think a professional manager would want to come all the way down here to train a load of llamas. Maybe we should start smaller . . . with someone who knows about football but lives near the farm?'

Tim grinned and did a small celebratory fist pump under the table. He knew Frank was on board with the idea now, even though he hadn't said it out loud yet.

'What about the team in the village?' suggested Monica. 'They could help out. They aren't very good though.'

'Doesn't matter,' said Tim. 'Our llamas are so good I reckon a monkey could manage them and they'd still beat a team of humans. It would be an amazing match.'

'Get a monkey manager,' shouted Fiona. 'I want a monkey manager.' She leaped up on her chair and started hopping about, making unusual screeching noises.

'That doesn't sound anything like a monkey,' said Beetroot calmly. 'Will you get down off your chair, Fiona?'

'I'm a monkey and I'm going to be the manager of the greatest football team ever!' Fiona hooted, hopping across to another chair and waving her arms about. 'Screech, screech! Whack the ball in the goal. Screech, screech! Cross it on my noggin . . .'

'Oh dear,' said Beetroot. 'I heard monkey football managers don't like ice cream for pudding. If only there was a polite little girl here who sat still; maybe she could have it instead.'

Fiona sat back down straight away and put on her best angelic look. The *Secret Rule Book of Being a Mum* is much more useful than the *Dad* one.

Frank stroked his bushy beard again. He liked seeing Tim happy. He was worried that moving to the farm and starting a new school had hit Tim the hardest, but the llamas had really perked him up. What harm could it do if he said yes? The chances of anyone actually agreeing to train the llamas were slim to none – but at least they could try, couldn't they?

Tim, Cairo, Monica and even Beetroot were now sitting expectantly waiting to see what Frank would say next.

'OK, let's find out the address of the local football team and go down there in the morning,' he announced. 'I think there's a chance we can get this idea to work. You'll still have to look after the llama poo though, Tim.'

Tim jumped up and started to do a little celebratory dance, then stopped. He *really* hated shovelling llama poo.

14
MEETING McCLOUD

On the other side of the village sat the home of the local football team, White Horse FC, which was named after the pub on the opposite side of the road. The pub was called the Red Lion . . . ha, ha, only kidding. It had one stand that held about a hundred people, which was unimaginatively called the White Horse Stand. Behind one goal was a huge quarry, which was full of footballs. The other two sides of the ground were just fields and a few houses. It was a typical ground, in a typical village . . . well, apart from the pond.

White Horse FC were not very good. Their top striker was fifty-five years old. I say top striker; he scored just four goals last season, and only two the season before. The other striker had scored just once in his entire life. He only had one nostril that worked properly, although this didn't make him any worse at football.

The two centre midfielders had been sent off ten times each this season – twice for fighting each other. The four defenders were brothers who loved swimming in the village pond, which had made them so stupid they kept forgetting what position they were playing in. It wasn't uncommon to find White Horse FC playing with three left backs during a match.

The majority of White Horse FC's victories came from own goals or the other team forgetting to turn up. Let's just say the standard of the league was really bad.

Tim, Frank and Cairo went down to the club an hour before White Horse FC were due to kick off one of their final games of the season, against top-of-the-table Wallop Town.

On the way, Tim and Cairo babbled excitedly about how the White Horse team would be thrilled to find out about their team of llamas. Even Frank found it hard not to join in with their enthusiasm.

Cairo had done some snooping on his phone to discover more about the White Horse manager, Steve Wharton, who he thought would be the best person to talk to about the llamas. He looked fairly young, with a neat, dark goatee beard, and always wore a baseball cap. Even in a picture of him celebrating with the players in a huge dirty bath, he was wearing a baseball cap. I'll tell you a secret: Steve was embarrassed about his bald patch, which is why he always wore a hat. Don't tell him I said that though; he's got a bit of a temper on him.

The trio found Steve Wharton sitting on a stool in the small team bar at the back of the White Horse Stand. He had his head in his hands. This was fairly common for Steve; he was an exceptionally grumpy man.

Tim felt all the enthusiasm drain out of him. Still, he was determined to do what was best for the llamas and the farm. He plucked up all the courage he could muster, marched up to the miserable-looking football manager and tried to win him round. 'We're from the farm on the other side of the village,' he said, his voice going a bit squeaky at the end. 'We've got something that you might want to come and see. It's amazing.'

Steve lifted his head out of his hands and stared at Tim with an uninterested expression. 'Go on.'

'We've got some llamas that are *really* good at football,' Tim continued nervously. 'Perhaps they could help out this football team?'

'They are probably the best footballers you are

ever likely to see,' added Cairo with a manic grin.

Steve smiled weakly, as though he'd just met three of the biggest nutters in the world and didn't want to do anything that might startle them. Very slowly, he stood up and started to back away towards the changing rooms. It wasn't really Steve's fault; finding out about a team of football-playing llamas is not something you encounter every day. 'That's really great to hear,' he said, nodding thoughtfully. 'But I've got a very important match in a bit and I need to get my team ready.' Then he legged it through the door.

'Oh dear, that didn't go very well, did it?' said a disappointed Frank. 'He must think we are barking mad.' He looked accusingly at Cairo, who was wearing a kilt for some reason.

Cairo wasn't barking mad, but he was a lazy dresser who wore the first thing he picked out of the cupboard each morning. This particular cupboard belonged to his Scottish uncle.

Tim was just about to suggest they chase after Steve when a sharp cough came from the corner of the room. Leaning on the bar was an old man in a cloth cap sawing away at a pineapple with a knife and fork.

'He's eating a pineapple with a knife and fork,' whispered Frank to Tim and Cairo through the corner of his mouth.

'Aye, that's the best way to do it, laddie. Ask anyone who lives near a pineapple tree,' said the man firmly, who despite being old could clearly hear perfectly well.

Tim, Cairo and Frank didn't know anyone who lived near a pineapple tree. Nobody lives near a pineapple tree; they don't grow on trees.

'So what's this I hear about llamas that can play football?' asked the man, stuffing some of the sharp green pineapple leaves into his mouth.

'He's eating

the leaves,' whispered Frank through gritted teeth to the boys.

'We HAVE got llamas that can play football!' cried Tim, ignoring his dad.

'The greatest footballers ever,' added Cairo.

The old man stopped chewing and his face became stern. 'Llamas you say . . . them things like camels?'

'They are part of the camel family, but they aren't camels,' said Cairo authoritatively.

'Good. I hates them camels,' grumbled the old man. 'Camels took my wife away from me.'

You would expect that he would go on to tell a long and rambling story about his wife and some camels, but he just stopped and took a large bite out of the rind of the pineapple instead. He swallowed with a grimace.

'These llamas are the best football–playing animals ever!' enthused Tim. 'You'd be amazed if you saw them.'

'Interesting,' said the old man. 'OK, I'll come and see these llamas.'

Tim was excited that *someone* wanted to see his llamas, but wasn't sure that a strange old man would be of any help. 'I'm sorry, but who actually are you?' he asked.

The old man looked slightly taken aback by an

eleven-year-old challenging his credentials.

'Well, sonny,' bristled the old man, 'let's just say I know a lot about football.' He threw a heavy medal on to the bar.

Tim picked it up and inspected it. 'Look, Dad! It's a World Cup winners' medal.'

'That's right sonny, I won the World Cup with Scotland, way back a long time ago.'

'Eh . . . that's not right,' interrupted Frank. 'Scotland has never won the World Cup.'

'Haven't they, laddie?' growled the old man. 'You clearly haven't been playing proper attention then, have yeh?'

'No . . .' replied Frank, frowning. 'I'm sure Scotland has never won the World Cup.'

'Dad, will you drop it,' hissed Tim. 'He knows about football and has a World Cup winners' medal – that's good enough for me.'

'Well done, son,' said the old man to Tim. 'Now let's go and see these llamas. You can call me McCloud by the way . . . car this way is it?' He left the bar and went outside.

Tim, Cairo and Frank stood in the empty clubhouse for a few minutes trying to soak up what had just happened.

'I think he's a bit bonkers,' said Frank quietly. 'We'll have to tell him that we're not interested in his help.'

'Why not?' asked Tim defiantly. 'I can't see anyone else offering to help us around here.'

'Plus he's got a World Cup medal,' added Cairo, who didn't really know what that was.

'That doesn't mean anything,' replied Frank with a sigh. 'He could have got that from a car-boot sale.'

'Well, I want to give him a try,' demanded Tim.

'Does the job for me,' added Cairo, sticking his thumbs up.

Frank stroked his beard and had a little think . . . which was a complete waste of time, as Tim and Cairo had already left the room to follow McCloud.

15
McCLOUD'S VERDICT

After five hours of watching the llamas pass, dribble, shoot, head, tackle and volley in the rain, McCloud returned to the farmhouse to pass his judgement. He was dripping wet and had a very stern look on his face. Tim could feel his heart fluttering as he waited for the verdict.

'What you have here is llamas . . . who can play football,' the old man said, taking a swig of cold tea from a mug Fiona had recently used as a paint pot. Luckily McCloud didn't notice.

'We know that,' said Tim, finding it hard not to feel exasperated. He had been expecting a less obvious statement.

'Ah, but what you don't know is, these llamas already have all the skills you'd expect of top international players. Like they've been taught everything overnight by the football gods, and we all know how strange the football gods can be, don't we?'

Tim, his dad and Cairo all nodded, indulging McCloud, but truth be told they hadn't a clue what he was banging on about.

'Any idea how they got so good?' asked McCloud.

'They are very rare llamas from the Andes; they are naturally good at it,' replied Tim, trying to keep his face as straight as he could.

Thankfully McCloud brushed off this feeble explanation as though it was completely normal. He believed that the world's best footballers are blessed with ability from birth, so it could easily happen to a llama. Plus, he'd never heard of the Andes.

'Of course, they've got no idea about tactics and formations,' he continued, 'but I can teach them that.'

'How would you do that?' asked Cairo. 'They are llamas after all. I'm a human and I don't know anything about tactics.'

'It's all about man-management and discipline,' McCloud snapped. 'Knowing when to give them the old hairdryer and when to put the old arm round the shoulder.'

Cairo was going to ask what the 'old hairdryer' was but thought better of it. What it really means is shouting at someone so hard that their hair is blown back like a hairdryer. Nasty.

'But these are llamas – not professional footballers. You can't apply the same rules to them, surely?' added Tim.

'That's true, laddie, but to be honest some of the footballers I've worked with in my fifty years in the game have no more common sense or brain power than some of these llamas. If I can train them, then I can train anything – whether it be a hippo, an anaconda, a Bengal tiger or a llama. Why, I've even heard about a tennis coach in Tibet who got some yaks to the Australian Open final. It's all about man-management, or in this case llama-management.'

Frank shot Tim an alarmed look.

The kind of look you give someone when you realize you have actually let someone completely mad into your kitchen. Surely no yak had ever reached a tennis final. McCloud didn't notice. He was already drawing formations and complicated diagrams on the back of one of Fiona's paintings, with arrows going this way and that. He was muttering, occasionally chuckling and then getting angry with himself. It was a little unsettling.

Frank decided he wanted this strange old man out of his house; he was clearly a few sandwiches short of a picnic. 'Shall we take you back to the football club, McCloud?' he suggested. 'It is getting rather late.'

'Aye, let's do that,' replied McCloud, putting the finishing touches to an unusual 2-6-2 tactic. 'There's a lot of work to be done here, mark my words. I'll give you a call when I've worked out a plan. I've got great hopes for these lads . . . I mean llamas.'

'Great, that's just great,' said Frank, pretending he believed everything McCloud was saying. As he shuffled him out of the door, Frank desperately hoped this would be the last time he ever saw the strange old Scotsman.

Sadly for Frank, he was wrong.

*

Tim and Cairo were waiting anxiously in the kitchen when Frank got back home from dropping off McCloud.

'Hi, Dad, how did it go?'

'I dropped him off, and he said he'd ring when he's got everything sorted,' said Frank with a sigh. 'He's clearly a fruitcake who thinks he knows everything about football.'

'For a moment I really thought he could help us make these llamas into a brilliant football team,' said Tim sadly, resting his chin on the table. 'But then he started talking about the yaks.'

'And doing all that mad tactic scribbling,' added Cairo.

'Yes, that was a bit of a worry,' replied Frank. 'There is no doubt the llamas are brilliant footballers, but to be honest they just charge about doing all their stuff. It would take some of the best animal trainers in the world years to get them to understand how to actually play the game.'

'So what do we do with the llamas then?' replied Tim, letting out a big sigh.

'Dunno,' said Frank shrugging. 'But we really need them to start making some money, as soon as possible.'

They sat in silence for a few minutes before Cairo piped up. 'Why don't we make the llamas, like, an attraction?' he said. 'You know, we'd charge people a pound or something to watch the llamas kick a football about?'

'Yeah, I suppose that's a pretty good idea,' said Frank unenthusiastically. 'But it's not going to make enough money to keep the farm going.' He pulled his black notepad out of his pocket and looked at it sadly.

Tim gritted his teeth and imagined throwing the notepad on a fire. What a disappointment the day had turned out to be.

'Ahem, ahem,' came a voice from the doorway. It was Monica holding her laptop, and she had a wry smile on her face. 'Don't you lot ever check anything on the internet? Look at this . . .' She turned the screen round and revealed a very blurry black-and-white picture of a man in a dark jersey diving full length to head a ball into the back of a net. Around him were loads of other players in white kits trying to stop it going in. Everyone in the picture looked about fifty years old. Their shorts were very short, they had huge sideburns and moustaches, and all of them had really badly styled hair.

Underneath the picture was a caption:

McCloud heads the winner against West Germany.

'I think you need to give McCloud a chance,' said Monica. 'He might be a bit eccentric, but he'll know more about football than the rest of you put together.'

Tim, Cairo and Frank studied the picture closely. You could just about make out McCloud's nose. Personally I never came across the fellow, or played against him. Our careers never really overlapped. This is why I haven't been very helpful up to this point, for which I can only apologize. Without Monica I also would have presumed he was an imposter.

'Wow, that's pretty impressive,' said Tim, putting his eyeball as close to the picture as possible.

'I know,' replied Cairo in awe. 'Especially as I've never heard of West Germany.'

16
A CALL IN THE NIGHT

Somehow, despite the amazing discovery of the football-playing llamas, the Gravy family managed to get on with their normal lives over the next few days. Tim, Fiona and Monica went back to school. Beetroot started volunteering in a charity shop, while also managing to fit in a punishing fitness regime. Frank continued to scribble angrily in his little black notepad, especially after he bought fresh hay and feed for the llamas. He was still struggling with Fiona's princess castle and had only reached chapter two of his beekeeping book. Tim toiled away shovelling llama poo into bags that nobody really wanted to buy.

The llamas continued to amaze the Gravy family with their skill, with Ludo standing to one side, watching but not getting involved. The llamas' coats were slowly getting healthier with all the fresh air and good food, and Frank had even started hoping that maybe they could start selling their wool before Christmas. McCloud seemed to have disappeared.

Until one night the phone rang . . .

Now, I'm not great with phones, as the nearest one to me when I was growing up was in a phone box at the bottom of the road, and I always hated those new-fangled mobile things. But even I know that a call at 2.46 a.m. is usually somebody with bad news.

'Frank Gravy?' came the muffled voiced at the other end.

'Er, yes,' said Frank wincing. He was waiting for bad news.

'It's McCloud.'

'Oh . . .' said Frank in confusion. 'Hello.'

'I've got some very, very, very good news,' said McCloud sternly, making it sound as if he was about to reveal the worst piece of news ever.

'Is this news so important that you have to tell me about it at two forty-six in the morning?'

'Oh aye, this is very, very, very good news . . . and it's actually five to three; your watch must be wrong.'

Frank sighed. 'OK, McCloud, what's the very, very, very good news then?'

There was a long pause from the other end of the

phone. 'We've been accepted to play in next season's Cup competition.'

'McCloud, I really don't care what happens to your football club, especially not at three in the morning!' started Frank.

'Not White Horse FC – those idiots can hardly lace up their boots!' interrupted McCloud. 'I'm talking about your llamas . . . I mean our llamas. Our llamas are going to be playing in the Cup next season. What do you think about that? I told you I'd sort something out.'

There was no reply.

'Gravy . . . Gravy . . . Gravy? What do you think about that?' shouted McCloud.

But there was still no reply, because Frank had put the phone down and gone back to bed thinking that McCloud must have eaten a really hot curry that had melted his brain.

But McCloud didn't stop ringing and ringing and ringing and ringing. Frank tried to ignore the calls, but eventually they had woken the entire family, which made him as unpopular as cold broccoli for breakfast. It was Tim who finally braved getting out of his nice, cosy, warm bed to pick up the phone.

'What are you playing at, man?' McCloud hooted

down the phone. 'We've been entered into the best cup competition in the entire world. We haven't got time for you to be horsing about like this. We've got to start training immediately! We've only got three months before it starts.'

'What's that?' asked Tim. 'Did you say we've been entered into the best cup competition in the world? Really the best cup in the world? The World Cup?'

'Oh, it's you, son.' McCloud's voice immediately calmed down. 'Well, not the World Cup, but it's the best domestic club knockout cup competition in the world. I've pulled a few strings and Llama United will be in the qualifying rounds. I've got an official letter from the Cup's governing body right here in my hand.'

'Wow, that's amazing . . . Hang on, did you say Llama United?'

'Aye, Llama United, that's what they're called.'

'Oh. Um . . . is there any way of changing it? Llama United is a bit boring.'

'It's not a pop group, sonny, and I couldn't call them Hippopotamus Albion or Bobcat Rovers, could I? It can't be changed now, it's official. The main thing is we are in the Cup.'

'Yes, yes, sorry, that is amazing.' Tim paused,

allowing the clever part of his brain to wake up and ask a question. 'Why have they let a team of llamas enter the Cup?'

McCloud went quiet for a bit. 'Well, I didn't actually tell them they were a team made up of llamas. We'll worry about that on the day of the first match. Right then, it's late and we need some rest. Big day tomorrow, first day of training. Pick me up at nine a.m. sharp,' ordered McCloud, and with that he put the phone down.

Tim crept into his parents' bedroom and flicked the lights on and off again about ten times, until his dad opened his eyes.

'What is it now?' Frank said eventually.

'That was McCloud. We are definitely going to play in the Cup. It's official; he's got the paperwork and everything,' said Tim, hopping up and down as though he was on springs. 'Oh and you've got to pick McCloud up for training at nine a.m.'

Frank desperately tried to think of reasons as to why this was a terrible idea – but Tim seemed so excited . . . he was so tired . . . and his pillow was so soft . . . that somehow he found himself growling, 'OK!'

'You're the best, Dad!' cried Tim, before running out of the room.

Frank pulled the duvet over his head. He was desperate to go back to sleep, he'd been dreaming about making some award-winning honey – but now all he could think about was the fact that he'd just agreed to let a mad old Scottish man train his llamas for a football cup. He groaned. His pillow *was* really soft though.

Tim returned to his room, frantically texted Cairo the good news, changed into his football training kit and boots and sat down on the edge of his bed to wait until 9 a.m., which was in about six hours' time. He didn't care; who needed sleep when there was football training to do?

17
TRAINING BEGINS

McCloud was waiting for Frank in the White Horse FC car park at 9 a.m. sharp. He was dressed from head to toe in an immaculate navy-blue velvet tracksuit. It had thin white piping down the shoulders, arms and legs, and a small bright-yellow badge with a red lion in the middle. On the back of the tracksuit, emblazoned in bold white writing, was the word SCOTLAND. He carried a brown briefcase-type thing in his left hand and a huge bag of football equipment in the other, crammed with cones, balls and flags. He checked his watch as Frank pulled into the car park and tutted.

'Yer four seconds late,' he grumbled as he got into Frank's car. 'I'll let you off this time, but don't let it happen again.'

'Again?' said Frank, stunned by the way McCloud was talking to him. He was starting to feel like the family butler. 'Am I going to have to pick you up every day until training is over?'

'Aye, that you will, sonny,' McCloud replied. 'But learn this one thing: training is never over. You have to eat, sleep and breathe football. If you are not thinking about it all the time, shame on you.' He wagged his finger aggressively at Frank, who tried to ignore it.

They drove in silence for a few minutes until Tim suddenly popped up in the back behind the driver's seat.

'Hullo,' he said breezily, which caused Frank to swerve on to the other side of the road.

'Why aren't you at school?' barked Frank as he pulled the car back into the correct lane of traffic.

'I'm the assistant manager. I can't miss the first day of training. School can wait.'

'It most certainly can't,' said Frank. He looked at Tim, who had his bottom lip out and was looking at him with his best begging eyes. 'OK, OK . . . you can do training today and at weekends, but you must be back at school from tomorrow.'

'What about afternoons?'

McCloud laughed. 'Afternoons? Afternoons! These llamas are going to be professional footballers . . . they don't need to train in the afternoons. They'll get all the training they need in the mornings and a few hours over the weekends.'

Tim slumped back in his seat in a huge sulk. They were his llamas and it was his idea to get them playing football. Now he wasn't allowed to help them train and he'd still have to go to that rotten school.

Frank dropped McCloud and Tim by the field and drove off to buy some more fresh hay and feed. He was also going to secretly look at beehives for the award-winning honey he hadn't made yet. Well, you've got to have dreams, haven't you?

McCloud stormed into the field and blew a small black whistle three times, then shouted words that Tim couldn't understand at the llamas.

The llamas stopped what they were doing, which was a mixture of chewing grass and some very short range passing, and looked at the Scottish coach.

'Right then, LLAMA UNITED,' McCloud bellowed. 'Get yourselves round me quickly.' He clapped his hands over his head three times.

One of the grey llamas snorted. The rest went back to munching on the grass. Only Ludo continued to stare at McCloud.

'HO! LLAMA UNITED, TO ME,' McCloud bellowed again.

The llamas still didn't move. Tim shrugged at McCloud, but he wasn't looking.

'LLAMAS TO ME, RIGHT NOOOWWWW!' McCloud really shouted this one, and his face went all purple.

Some of the llamas took a step back. Others started to huddle together, glancing suspiciously in McCloud's direction.

'Right, I'll show them who's boss,' muttered McCloud under his breath, and he sprinted towards the llama closest to him.

Tim had never seen a man as old as McCloud sprint. The bottom half of his body was a whir of legs, while the top half remained perfectly still

103

with his arms firmly planted by his sides. Tim covered his mouth so McCloud wouldn't see him laughing.

McCloud reached the closest llama and grabbed its hindquarters in an effort to turn it round to face the middle of the field. But the llama was having none of it and kicked out its back legs, sending McCloud crashing to the floor. McCloud wasn't a man who gave up easily. He tried again and again and again and again and again and again and again and again, but each time with the same result – he was kicked, butted or knocked unceremoniously to the ground. His lovely navy-blue velvet tracksuit was covered in mud.

'Hey, assistant manager,' he barked at Tim as he picked himself up off the floor. 'You get these llamas to come to the middle of the field so I can train them.'

'But I don't know how!' said Tim.

'Just try, laddie,' cried McCloud, puffing and wheezing. 'I'm out of ideas.'

Tim gingerly approached the nearest group of llamas. He thought talking to them nicely would probably work best. 'Ahem, excuse me llamas. Would you mind following me to the middle of the field so we can train you to play in the Cup?'

The llamas looked at Tim briefly through bemused eyes, then once again returned to their grass chomping.

Tim tried snapping his fingers, clapping his hands, waving his arms and making shoo-shooing noises, but nothing seemed to register even a glimmer of interest with the llamas. He really needed Cairo's help for this; he'd know what to do.

In frustration Tim booted a ball high into the air and towards the middle of the field. The llamas looked up from their incessant chomping and followed the path of the ball with their eyes. As the ball landed and bounced, every single one of them except Ludo broke into a canter and charged after the ball, which also happened to mean they were running towards McCloud, who was lying flat on his back after his last llama-induced tumble. The old Scotsman just had time to see the ball bounce casually past him before ten llamas charged over him, knocking him unconscious.

When McCloud came around, Tim was standing over him flapping a towel at his face . . . he'd seen people do this in films when someone had been knocked out.

'It's the ball, McCloud!' he cried as he flapped. 'The ball! They are only really bothered about the ball. That's how we can train them.'

'Aye, lad,' replied McCloud groggily. 'That's all the greats cared about, the ball and nothing else. I think we might have to start training them in the afternoons, after school, so you and your little friend can help me. What do you think?'

'Yes please!' cried Tim, his heart fluttering with excitement. 'Cairo would love to help, he knows everything about llamas.'

'We could get your mother involved too,' McCloud added, squelching in the mud as he tried and failed to sit up, 'as a fitness trainer. She seems to spend a lot of time doing press-ups and squat thrusts. Perhaps she could create a routine that will make the lads fitter? They'll need to be at peak physical fitness to compete at the top level.'

Tim nodded eagerly. Leaving McCloud to pull himself out of the mud, he ran off to find Beetroot. She would be thrilled that she would finally have something to train, even if it was a herd of llamas. For the first time in a long time, Tim felt that something was finally going his way.

*

Tim and McCloud spent the rest of the day working non-stop with the llamas. Shooting drills, passing drills, cone routines, dead balls, sprints, tactical positions, the list of stuff they needed to practise was endless.

Cairo appeared at mid-afternoon to offer some friendly support and advice on llama care. He also brought a large pair of nail clippers with him.

'I think this why they are puncturing so many balls,' he explained to Tim. 'Nobody has clipped their toenails for ages. They'll be like daggers by now. You'll need to come and help me though.'

Tim looked down at one of the llama's feet. Cairo was right, their toenails did look incredibly long and sharp. He was glad he had such a resourceful friend. It would save them a small fortune in burst footballs, something that would also make his dad happy.

Tim escorted the first pair of llamas towards Cairo and his clippers, using a mixture of hay, the ball, some friendly strokes and the odd pat as a lure. They seemed fairly happy to be separated from the rest of the herd, almost skipping along by Tim's side. He was really getting used to being around the llamas now. They didn't flinch when he touched them and occasionally they'd give him a playful nudge with their heads.

'Who are these two fine ladies then?' enquired Cairo giving the small sandy-coloured pair with little white socks a friendly pat on the neck.

'Er, ladies?' said Tim in confusion. 'I thought all of them were boys.'

'Nah, you've definitely got some girl llamas here,' said Cairo, readying his clippers.

'Ah, I was going to call them Dasher and Lightning, because they are the fastest and best crossers we have, but they aren't really girls' names, are they? We should change them.'

'Just because they are girls it doesn't mean you have to change their names. They are perfect names, even if they do sound a little bit like Father Christmas's reindeer.'

'I didn't know girls could be this good at football,' said Tim thoughtfully.

'Well, I don't know anything about football,' said Cairo, bending down to inspect Dasher's front nails. 'But if someone is a good footballer, it doesn't matter if they are girl or a boy. As long as they help the team win matches, who cares?'

Cairo carefully trimmed Dasher and Lightning's

toenails while stroking and humming to them in a reassuring manner. 'This is going to take ages,' he said, when he'd finished. 'Why don't you write me down a list of the llamas' names, what they look like, positions and what they are like, so I can go round and tidy them all up. Then you can get back to training.'

'Why do you need to know their positions and what they are like?' asked Tim.

'I want to learn more about them. They all have their own personalities, just like people. You'd be surprised how different they can be.'

'Suppose so,' said Tim, taking out a scrap of paper and a pen. He began drawing up a team sheet.

I've copied it out for you below, and corrected all the bad spelling, as Tim's a terrybull speller.

DEFENDERS

BRIAN

Grey, large black patch on body. Biggest and cleverest defender. Best at heading. He's the leader at the back and takes himself very seriously. Gets angry if others make a mistake.

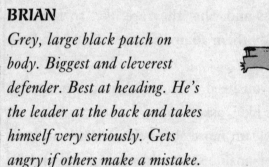

BILL

Grey, four black patches on body. Second biggest defender, but not as clever as Brian. Bit clumsy, which makes him a bit of a fouler . . . probably does most of the biggest poos.

BOB

Grey all over, no patches. Doesn't seem to be that confident, always stays close to Brian. Brilliant dribbler. Likes looking at his own reflection in the water trough, because he has such an amazing haircut.

BARCELONA

Grey all over, with black ears and chin. Runs with his tongue hanging out. Excellent at slide tackles. Really enjoys himself when playing, seems really cheerful.

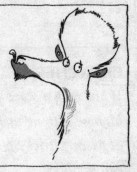

MIDFIELDERS

DASHER

Sandy coloured all over, four white socks, small, fast and really good at crossing. Loves to run at defenders and beat them for skill.

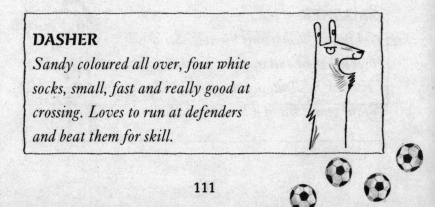

LIGHTNING

Sandy coloured all over, two white socks on front feet, small, fast and really good at crossing. Green eyes. Great positional awareness, always seems to arrive at exactly the right place at the right time.

CRUNCHER

White with a black flash across his nose. Strong tackler, good at passing, tricky feet. Will eat anything.

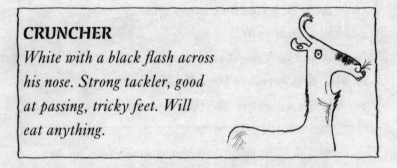

SMASHER

White, no flash across his nose. Strong tackler, good passer, powerful shot. The tough, silent, defensive midfielder of the team. Bit of a beard.

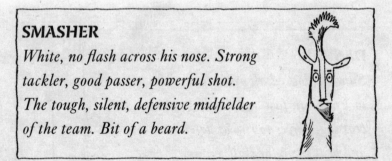

STRIKERS

THE DUKE

Brown and white, incredibly tall, powerful neck, great at headers. Always holds his head high like he's posh. Has a high opinion of himself.

GOAL MACHINE

Totally white with a light grey flash across his nose, ugly teeth sticking out over his bottom lip. Sparkly eyes a bit too close together. Best shooter in the team; the one who'll score all the goals.

When Cairo had finished he returned to Tim and threw him a bag full of llama toenails. 'Looks like Cairo's Nail Salon is closed for another day,' he said, letting out a puff of air as though he'd been working a twenty-hour shift in a Victorian pottery factory.

'Thanks Cairo, they all look really smart,' said Tim, having an idea. 'Hey, why don't you be our first-team physio?'

Cairo puffed out his chest with pride. 'That, I can do.'

'That's great! Welcome to the team, Mr Physio,' said Tim, shaking Cairo enthusiastically by the hand.

Cairo started to do an unnecessary warm-up routine, which included five star jumps, two feeble press-ups and one awful sit-up, which made him cry out in pain, as though it was the toughest thing ever. 'I think I've identified a bit of a problem boss,' he puffed as he began jogging on the spot.

'What's that?' asked Tim, his eyes fixed on Goal Machine, who had just powered home an incredible header.

'Well, as you know, I'm no football expert, but where's your goalkeeper?'

18
THE KEEPER

Cairo was right. Despite the best efforts of Tim and McCloud, the most crucial position on the pitch remained unfilled. They'd put all ten llamas in goal, but none had shown any interest in stopping a ball being shot at them. They either ran out of goal to chase the ball, leaving an empty net, or ducked out of the way. To be fair, being a goalkeeper isn't fun. You get really muddy, everyone shouts at you when you make a mistake, and if your team score you are so far away you can't really celebrate. This is why I always played inside right. That's a position from a long time ago. I suppose you would call me an attacking midfielder now.

'Have you tried Ludo in goal?' asked Cairo, pointing at the big black llama.

'Ludo has no interest in the ball or the game,' replied Tim with a sigh. 'He just stands there –

looking down the road.'

Cairo rubbed his chin. 'Remember I told you about guard llamas, and how they like to protect things?'

'I suppose so,' said Tim with a shrug, pretending he hadn't forgotten . . . which he had.

'Well, maybe he'd guard the net, if you asked him nicely?' Cairo suggested.

'Why me? *You're* the llama expert.'

'Ah, but he likes you,' replied Cairo. 'You're easily his favourite.'

'Am I?' said Tim, secretly pleased Cairo had noticed this.

'Of course. When he is not looking down the road, he is always glancing back to see where you are.' Cairo smiled and ran off to collect Ludo from the side of the field.

Tim stopped McCloud's how-to-dish-out-a-crafty-kick-on-the-opposition-striker-during-the-first-corner-of-the-match session and explained the Ludo plan. McCloud frowned and crossed his arms, clearly unimpressed.

Once Ludo was in front of the net, Cairo joined Tim and McCloud on the edge of the penalty area they'd marked out around the goal.

'Right then,' said McCloud. 'Let's see if this one

can stop any of these.' He smashed a low ball into the corner of the net. Ludo watched casually as it rolled past him.

'Hmmmmm. Maybe that was too hard for a first-timer,' continued McCloud, as he lightly tapped the ball towards the other corner of the net. Once again Ludo watched the ball creep past him.

'OK, let's try one right at him,' said McCloud firmly. Tim could sense McCloud was getting frustrated now. McCloud smashed the ball straight at the llama and unsurprisingly it hit him square on the chest and bounced away. Ludo snorted loudly in disgust and trotted out of the net and back to the other side of the field.

'I don't think he's much of a goalkeeper,' said Cairo unhelpfully.

'Ach! Red Lichties!' shouted McCloud, booting a cone towards a huddle of llamas nearby. 'We are going to get knocked out in the first match because we can't find a goalkeeper. All this work for nothing.'

Tim was just working up the courage to tell McCloud off for kicking a cone, when he noticed Ludo doing something out the corner of his eye. 'Look at that!' he exclaimed, pointing at the huge black llama, who was sprinting down the field to stand in front of

117

the llamas who'd had the cone kicked towards them.

'Of course!' exclaimed Cairo. 'He needs something to guard, something alive! Not a goal. That's not real to a llama, but he will protect the other llamas. Quick, let's get one in the back of the net and test it out.'

McCloud grabbed the unsuspecting Barcelona, who seemed to be in the middle of an attempted moonwalk, and led him to the back of the goal.

'OK, let's try it now,' said Tim, and he fired a shot straight at Barcelona. The ball powered through the air – Tim had hit it really well and it was bang on target. It was just about to strike poor Barcelona, when Ludo sprang into action, diving across the goal to knock the ball away with its head. What a save!

McCloud tried it again and the result was the same, another brilliant save.

McCloud, Tim and Cairo stood there, totally stunned for a few seconds, and then burst out laughing and cheering.

'We've done it laddies, the final piece of the jigsaw!' cried McCloud with a laugh as he high-fived Tim and Cairo before grabbing them both in a massive hug.

But Tim had one thought nagging away at the back of his mind. 'We've still got a problem,' he said, struggling out of McCloud's embrace. 'We can't leave Barcelona in goal for Ludo to protect. We need him in defence.'

McCloud squinted into the distance. 'Aye, that is a problem. We'll have to find something else for Ludo to guard.' He rubbed the side of his face for a good few minutes before a wicked grin flashed across his face. 'Why don't you go in goal, sonny?'

Tim frowned. 'What? I'm not doing that, it'll hurt.'

'No, it won't,' said the Scotsman encouragingly. 'Your llama pal will save every shot. Go on, give it a try.'

'Sounds like a good idea. I might even have a shot,' said Cairo, rubbing his hands together with glee.

Tim dropped his shoulders and stomped over to the goal. He knew this wasn't going to be fun.

'You'll stop this won't you, Ludo?' said Tim to the llama as he walked past. Ludo didn't react – he was busy nibbling on a huge dandelion.

McCloud fired in a powerful piledriver from the edge of the area. Tim could hear the ball making a high-pitched singing noise as it flew through the air then, WHACK . . . it hit him smack bang in the face. His nose decided this really wasn't a fun game and exploded with blood. Ludo, who hadn't moved at all, looked at Tim like he was the biggest idiot in the world for standing somewhere where balls were being kicked at him and carried on munching his dandelion.

Tim let out a yelp and grabbed his bleeding nose as Cairo ran across to him with a handful of dirty-looking tissues. It was his first proper job as team physio and he was excited. He did an unhelpful 'nee-naw-nee-naw' ambulance noise as he ran.

'Maybe putting you in goal isn't the best idea,' said McCloud thoughtfully from the edge of the area. 'We'll have to think of something else.'

Cairo slowly wiped the remaining bits of blood from around Tim's nose. He wasn't really concentrating. Every dab was getting slower and slower; he was clearly thinking about something else. 'Of course,' he said, clicking his fingers. 'I knew it! I knew it!'

'Knew what?' mumbled Tim through a wad of bloody tissues.

'We've got a sheep back at the shelter.'

'A sheep?'

'Guard llamas will protect sheep; we can just stick it in the goal. Wow, I am brilliant sometimes.' Cairo gleefully patted himself on the back.

'And you couldn't have thought about the sheep before I got my nose bashed in?' Tim's whole face was still buzzing from the whack, and he was a bit annoyed that Cairo was busy congratulating himself while he was in so much pain.

'Oh yes, sorry. Sometimes my genius ideas do take a bit of time to get to the front of my brain.'

Tim sat down and lay back on the grass, holding his nose as high as he could to stop the nose bleed. A shadow appeared over his head. It was McCloud.

'What you doing on the floor, sonny?'

'My nose hurts,' Tim whined.

'No time for noses; they are overrated,' the Scotsman roared. 'Go and get that sheep.'

19
MOTORWAY

Tim and Cairo had to wait until the next day to get the sheep, as it was getting dark. Then Tim had to go to school, which made it seem like the slowest day ever. He learned about peaches, and which sauce goes best with them. The whole school voted for mint sauce, including Fiona, and they all laughed in his face when he suggested that cream was the normal option. They called him 'mouldy cream boy' for the rest of the day.

Cairo was feeding a tortoise a massive lettuce leaf when Tim finally got to the animal shelter. There was a tiny nibble mark on one edge of the leaf.

'I've been feeding Clive this lettuce for five hours now,' Cairo sighed, nodding at the tortoise. Clive is a big name for things with a shell. Every single lobster in the world is called Clive, which is incredibly confusing. Shout 'Clive' at a tank of lobsters and they'll all turn round. 'But he seems happy enough, so I'm OK with it.'

'That's great,' replied Tim, not really listening. 'Have you got the sheep then?' He had been thinking about it most of the day and was keen to see what it looked like. As I'm sure you'll know, most sheep look exactly the same, but Tim had never seen one close up and he was really excited about it.

Cairo put the lettuce leaf down, just as Clive was about to take his biggest mouthful of the day. 'She's in our field round the back. Come with me.'

Cairo's 'round the back' was very different from what you and I would call 'round the back'. The field was about a mile away, across a boggy marsh that Tim nearly lost one of his school shoes in.

Scrunched in one corner of the long thin field were five black-and-white cows all sitting down as though they were on holiday in Spain. At the very far end was one solitary sheep looking very, very grumpy. The main part of the field was dominated by two angry-looking goats, who were patrolling it like guard dogs.

'So, we ignore the goats,' said Cairo in a nervous sing-song voice, as he hurdled the fence in one bound. 'We ignore the goats . . . we don't look at the goats . . . nothing to see here, goats. Just two boys crossing your field. Ignore the goats, Tim. Don't look at the goats. Whatever you do, *don't look at the goats*.'

Tim followed closely, almost clipping the heels of Cairo's mismatched wellingtons. Being instructed to not look at the goats made him want to look at the goats even more. He tried to focus on the back of Cairo's head instead.

After a very stressful couple of minutes they finally reached the sheep.

'She's called Motorway,' called Cairo. ''Coz we found her by the side of a motorway, covered in soot and exhaust fumes. She was pretty much all black by the time we got to her.'

'She doesn't look very happy in this field.'

'Nah, she doesn't. We think she might miss the roar of car engines charging past. It's too quiet for her here.' Cairo gave the sheep something orange out of his pocket, probably a carrot – I couldn't quite see. I was distracted by the goats.

'Hello, Motorway,' bellowed Cairo at the top of his voice. 'How are you today?' He turned to Tim. 'You say something, but make sure you shout. She likes that.'

'Er . . . lovely weather we are having, eh, Motorway?' Tim shouted.

Both Cairo and Motorway gave Tim a funny look.

'We are going to take you to help our football team,' Cairo bellowed. 'Motorway, you are going to play a vital part in the team.'

'She's only going to stand in the net,' muttered Tim.

'*Sssssshhh*,' hissed Cairo, pulling Tim to one side. 'Don't say things like that! She thinks she's a princess.'

'*A princess?*'

'Yes. If you want her to help us you have to treat her with respect, bow and do other things you would do with a princess. She's very elegant.'

Tim looked at Motorway. She didn't look very elegant to him. She looked like a sheep. Although he did notice that despite being in a really muddy field, she was very neat and tidy – not a speck of dirt on her and her hair was bright white.

'You'll get on well with my little sister; she thinks she's a princess too,' yelled Tim to Motorway.

Cairo pulled a purple silk scarf from one of his many pockets and carefully tied it loosely around the sheep's neck. 'Now, Motorway, if you'd be so good as to follow us to meet the other members of your football team, that would be very gracious of you,' shouted Cairo. 'But once again, everyone, we are ignoring the goats. Tum-tee-tee . . . *ignoring the goats*.'

Motorway followed Cairo at a leisurely trot, with her head held high as though she was acknowledging an invisible crowd that were clamouring to see her. Tim followed but every time he went ahead, Motorway would give him a piercing stare, forcing him to drop back.

So the whole of Tim's long walk home was looking at the backside of a sheep, whilst desperately trying not to look at the goats.

If you've ever had the misfortune to stare at a sheep's bottom, you'll know it's an unpleasant experi—

OH NO! I LOOKED AT A GOAT!

20
PRE-SEASON TRAINING

The qualifying rounds of the Cup started in late August, so Tim, Cairo and McCloud spent the whole summer training the llamas and Motorway. It was tough going, but they were making real progress. Motorway's presence in the goal worked perfectly. Ludo could think of nothing more important than protecting her from being hit by the ball. If occasionally he was beaten he would fume outwardly, spit on the floor and dig his feet into the ground, making him even more determined not to let another goal in.

Cairo made the goal look like a palace for Motorway, with purple ribbons, bunting that he'd coloured in with a gold pen, and a plush cushion. He'd even brushed Ludo's hair all smart so he looked like her butler. At first Ludo didn't enjoy this, but after Tim brushed his own hair into the same style to show it was OK, the big llama agreed to the change with his now customary nod.

The draw for the opening rounds of the Cup had been made, and Llama United were playing at home to a team called Brocket Town. In these early stages of the competition it wasn't much of a surprise if you'd never heard of the opposition. The league teams didn't join until the first round in November, while the biggest teams only started playing in the third round in January. Brocket Town could have been from just down the road or on the Scottish border for all Tim knew. To be honest, I've no idea where Brocket is either.

There was just one small problem. Nobody apart from McCloud, Cairo, Cairo's mum and the Gravy family had any idea that Llama United was actually a team of llamas. Most people thought it was just a wacky name for a new up-and-coming team. White Horse FC had even agreed to let them play their home matches on their pitch. It would bring in welcome extra money from supporters coming to the ground, both through the turnstiles and in the bar and burger stand during the match.

The family had really pulled together as the new season drew closer. Monica, Beetroot and Cairo's mum, Molly, had come up trumps with the kit. It was a purple stripy top that the llamas would wear over their hindquarters like a coat; they all had numbers stitched on the side. Beetroot had also drawn up plans for some stripy Llama United scarves. Apart from all the sewing, she'd been incredibly busy with her llama fitness regime. She was up first thing every morning warming up the llamas, testing their stamina levels and checking their sprint times. She regularly provided McCloud and Tim with complicated spreadsheets full of times and distances. The two girls, Dasher and Lightning, were easily the quickest over a hundred metres, while Smasher was the toughest when it came to the long runs. He never seemed to get out of breath.

Monica built a really cool website called llamaunited.com with loads of information and pictures about the team and the family, which they planned to launch after the first match so they wouldn't give away the big secret. Frank also seemed to be a bit happier. He had struck a deal with White Horse FC to get some of the money from the ticket sales for the home Cup matches. He knew it wouldn't be a lot, but it might help keep the bank from taking the farm away for a few more weeks. He'd also read up to chapter four in his beekeeping book and built two walls of Fiona's princess castle.

Even McCloud had done his bit. He'd bought himself and the boys a huge pile of chewing gum to chomp through during the match. Chewing gum seems to be the main thing modern football managers do these days while they are in the dugout or technical area, along with pointing, clapping, hopping up and down, tearing at their hair and dancing . . . well, perhaps not dancing.

So what had Fiona been up to? Well, she was in the thick of all the action, the boss of all the projects, although she didn't ever do any actual work. She pointed, made suggestions, had opinions, shook her head, folded her arms and told everyone how to do things better. She also drank a staggering amount of juice, because nobody was keeping an eye on how many times she went to the fridge.

21
LLAMA UNITED V
BROCKET TOWN

The sun was shining as Tim, Cairo, Frank and the llamas drove up to the back of White Horse FC stadium. Frank had borrowed Molly's animal transporter, which she'd said they could use for the duration of the cup run. Molly was generous like that.

Tim could feel his stomach flipping over and over with a mixture of nerves and excitement, while his hands were unusually sweaty. McCloud was waiting in the car park with the doors to the ground wide open. He didn't want anyone to see the llamas before kick-off, just in case someone complained and they weren't allowed to take the field. There are always busybodies that go out of their way to ruin everyone's fun, and McCloud didn't want to encounter any of these types before the llamas had even got their kit on.

White Horse FC was expecting a bumper crowd

for the first match of the Cup . . . of about forty-five people. Which was *at least* ten more than usual; four of them being Beetroot, Monica, Fiona and Molly, all of whom had never been to a game before. Actually Molly had once seen an international friendly, but it was a very boring 0 – 0 draw, so she'd wiped it from her mind.

The llamas were led into the small changing rooms by Tim and Cairo with the help of a load of hay. Once in the changing rooms they all quickly realized that hiding in here for a few hours before the game was going to be a nightmare. The llama poo was already beginning to pile up on the floor, and you could hardly move without a llama head, neck or body getting in the way. So they led the llamas back to the relative comfort of the transportation van and waited until just before kick-off to run on to the playing field.

Brocket Town were already on the pitch dressed in a full yellow kit, which was so bright it was actually hard to look at any of their players for longer than about ten seconds.

'Right, this is it, llamas,' bellowed McCloud, marching up and down inside the transportation van as he spoke. 'This is the big moment. Go out there

133

and give it your best, but most of all, win this for yourselves.'

The llamas looked blankly at their Scottish boss. They had no idea what he was talking about.

Then Frank opened the van doors and Tim, Cairo and McCloud bravely led the llamas around the side of the stand and on to the pitch, while Frank went and positioned himself just behind the rickety dugouts. There was a huge gasp from the crowd. Well, as loud a gasp as forty-five . . . no, forty-nine people can make. Four more people had popped in at the last minute as they were passing by on their way to the shops.

Tim overcame his nerves and grinned from ear to ear. He'd been looking forward to this all summer and had been running this moment over and over in his mind for weeks. The plan was to appear as cool and casual as possible, as though managing a team of llamas was a normal everyday event.

As soon the captain of Brocket Town saw the llamas, he stormed straight up to the referee, who was standing in the middle of the pitch with his mouth wide open.

'What the Austrian coffee cake is this?' the captain shouted. He worked as a mechanic during the week;

the garage was next to a bakery.

The referee took a little bit of time to compose himself and then muttered, 'It looks like a team of llamas to me.'

'We can't play a team of llamas,' yelled the Brocket Town captain, stamping his feet on the ground like a three-year-old. 'It's . . . not . . . fair!'

'I'm not sure there is anything about it in the rules,' said the referee with a frown.

'I don't *care* about the rules; we are not playing a team of llamas!'

Now anyone who plays football knows that the worst thing you can ever say to a referee is 'I don't care about the rules'; it's plain madness.

Spurred on by the captain's flagrant disregard for everything he stood for, the ref snapped: 'Well, I can tell you what the rules *do* say: if you don't play the game, you forfeit the match.'

Realizing the referee was serious, the disgruntled captain stomped off towards his team. The crowd of forty-nine started to boo and hiss; they wanted to see the llamas play.

'Hello ref, how are you diddle-ing today?' said Cairo casually as he passed him to tie Motorway to one of the nets and decorate her mini-palace. The referee opened and closed his mouth a few times but no words came out, his mind had gone to mush.

'We OK to get going in a bit?' Tim asked eagerly. 'It is their debut after all, and some of them are a bit nervous.' He pointed at a huge pile of poo that had appeared next to Bill.

'Er . . . er . . . yes, I suppose so,' said the ref, checking his watch. 'I'm just waiting for the other team to decide if they're playing or not.'

The Brocket Town captain made his way back to the centre circle. 'OK, OK – we'll play the game. It should be fairly easy to beat a team of llamas anyway.'

Some of you might be thinking, hey why is the captain making all the decisions? Unusually, as well as being a mechanic, he's also the player-manager and the club owner. Which made him rather big-headed and impossible to substitute.

The referee blew his whistle to start the game and Brocket Town kicked off. They played the ball around among themselves for a few seconds, then, boringly, all the way back to the keeper. The crowd booed. The keeper passed it to the left back, who jogged with the ball all the way up to the halfway line where he was promptly tackled by Cruncher, who then cantered towards the Brocket goal, unchallenged, and slammed the ball past the keeper from twenty yards out.

1 – 0 to Llama United in the first minute!

The Brocket team were so stunned they looked like a team of statues. A team of statues that were pointing in disbelief with their mouths open wide.

Tim suddenly forgot his 'play it cool' plan, leaped as high as he could and punched the air. Cairo did exactly the same. McCloud didn't move; he just tapped his watch and muttered, 'Long way to go yet, boys.'

The game continued like this for nearly the whole first half. Brocket Town were so shocked they could hardly cross the halfway line, and every time they did they were tackled, which usually resulted in one of the llamas having a shot from varying angles and distances. Luckily for Brocket Town, their keeper was one of the few players actually having a good game. He made twenty-seven saves and only let in six.

Yes, it was Llama United 6 – 0 Brocket Town at half-time.

Brocket hadn't had a single shot on goal. Ludo and Motorway were so bored they'd eaten all the grass in the goalmouth by the time the referee blew his whistle for the break.

Llama United stayed on the pitch during half-time. A proud Tim and Cairo wandered among them, giving them water from a couple of buckets, but they didn't really need it as they had hardly run about at all. Meanwhile there was an almighty noise coming from the Brocket Town changing room; they were having a huge row and probably a massive punch-up.

When the second half started, Brocket Town had clearly changed their tactics, expecting the llamas to have a bad goalkeeper. This meant they started shooting from long range. I mean really, really long range . . . as in from-their-own-half range. It didn't do them much good – most of the shots either didn't have the power to reach the Llama United goal or lacked accuracy and the balls would go high and wide. The few balls that did reach Ludo were just nodded away with his head or tapped to the side with his foot. A man in the crowd starting singing 'England's number one, England's, England's number one!' but nobody else joined in.

When the final whistle came the score was 17 – 0. The Brocket Town keeper had hurt his hand and bashed his head in the half-time punch-up, so didn't have as good a second half. It was a total trouncing. Goal Machine scored seven, the Duke five, Cruncher two, and one each for Dasher, Lightning and Brian, who powered home a towering header from a corner. Cruncher even created his own special kind of goal celebration. He'd strut over to the corner flag and take a huge bite out of it. Although maybe it wasn't a celebration; perhaps he was just hungry.

Tim, Cairo and McCloud danced wildly across the pitch, weaving in and out of the llamas and the beaten Brocket Town players, who were covering their faces in embarrassment. The llamas didn't celebrate; they just stood about munching grass. It was particularly tasty at the White Horse ground.

The forty-nine people in the crowd couldn't believe what they'd just witnessed; well, apart for

Molly, Beetroot, Monica and Fiona, who were all cheering wildly. Most of the rest of the crowd had watched the first half in stunned silence, as though they were sitting in the middle of a dream. But by the second half a few people had taken their phones out and were taking pictures and videos and posting them online. The secret was out – Llama United were going to become famous . . . very quickly.

'Don't get carried away, laddie,' cautioned McCloud to Tim in the van on the way back to the farm. 'That will be the worst team we face, plus we had the added shock factor. As soon as everyone else in the Cup finds out there is a brilliant team of football-playing llamas in the game, it's going to get a lot trickier. The other teams will have their tactics ready. From now on we need to train harder than ever before.'

22
PIRTSMOUTH V
LLAMA UNITED

The grainy videos and pictures of Llama United smashing Brocket Town in the first qualifying round went viral, and had been viewed all over the world by the end of the weekend. It was phenomenal. Monica's new website had thousands of hits and the local media started ringing the farm demanding interviews.

As you and I don't have the time to go through every qualifying match individually, I will show you the local sport headlines from the next few games. You can add music if you want, like TV shows do when they're rounding things up. Not hip-hop, though . . . I still don't know what that is.

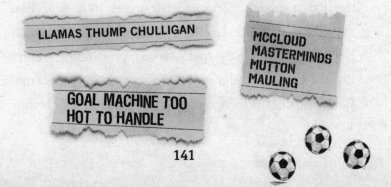

LLAMAS THUMP CHULLIGAN

MCCLOUD MASTERMINDS MUTTON MAULING

GOAL MACHINE TOO HOT TO HANDLE

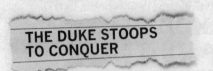
They weren't actually on fire; this is just lazy football-headline writing, and actually means 'played really well'.

Llama United were unstoppable, and the mixture of amateur and semi-professional teams from the lower leagues that they were drawn against couldn't handle them. They were smashed by the rampaging llamas. Not one team managed to score a goal, and all of them let in ten or more. It was just too easy. Goal Machine and the Duke were a lethal partnership up front, Dasher and Lightning gave full backs nightmares, Smasher and Cruncher were a formidable midfield duo, and Bob's hair continued to look amazing. The defence and Ludo had so little to do, you sometimes forgot they were actually on the pitch.

Tim, Cairo and McCloud were becoming quite the experienced management team. It looked like they'd been doing this for years. Back at the farm Beetroot and Molly had started producing Llama United scarves and a range of kits to sell to the fans. Beetroot's cardio workouts managed to make Dasher and Lightning even faster, and Smasher as strong as a tank. Frank continued to spend his time anxiously scribbling sums in his little black notepad, but did manage to afford to buy a beekeeper's hat and six bees, who all escaped. Monica also taught Fiona that lemon sherbet shouldn't be added to lasagne.

In November, the draw for the first round of the Cup was announced; this is when League teams are entered into the competition for the first time. Llama United were drawn against League Two side Pirtsmouth, a team who'd won the Cup twice in their history. Even though they were a bit down on their luck, they still had a huge fanbase and some very experienced players. What was different this time was that Pirtsmouth were drawn at home. It would be Llama United's first match away from the relative familiarity of the White Horse Stadium.

McCloud was worried, but then again he had worried about every single round so far. Tim was much more confident . . . until the llama transportation vehicle pulled into the car park of Pirtsmouth's ground after a long five-hour drive. 'Wow, this ground is huge,' he said with a gulp. His tummy did a nervous flip.

It was the biggest ground he'd ever seen, with four

huge stands, massive floodlights, turnstiles, bars, an army of food vans and a throng of people wandering about before the match started. It was going to a big game, not just for Llama United but for Pirtsmouth too. The national media had turned out in force because this was the kind of ground that could handle large numbers of journalists and TV camera crews.

Everyone wanted to see Llama United win; everyone, that is, except for the Pirtsmouth fans. A defeat to a team of llamas would be totally humiliating for a professional football team.

'Bah,' McCloud scoffed. 'This ground is tiny – it only holds about twenty thousand people. Some grounds can take sixty, seventy or even eighty thousand spectators. In the World Cup I played in front of over one hundred thousand people in Mexico City. Scored three goals . . . two of the best you'll ever see in your life.'

Frank, who was driving the transporter, let out a huge sigh. Over the last few months it had been exhausting trying to keep up with McCloud's raft of footballing stories and anecdotes. The old picture Monica had found online clearly showed that McCloud had played at least one international game. But wow, he really did bang on about how brilliant he had been. Frank was sick of it, so he turned up the radio to listen to the commentators talk about today's match instead:

'Let's go to Frittan Park now, where the surprise package of the Cup, Llama United, get to test themselves against a professional team for the first time. Dave Dunk is there for us,' rambled the first man.

'That's right, Mark. Llama United have certainly been the big story of the Cup this year. Eleven actual llamas and a sheep, managed by an old man and two kids, have literally stunned the world of football with their mix of skill and ruthlessness in front of goal. This afternoon we'll find out whether the farmyard amateurs have enough in them to beat the professionals from the coast. This is Man versus Beast, on a football field, and it's here live from three p.m. on Radio Shouty. Back to you Mark.'

The crowd was really loud as Tim, Cairo and McCloud led the llamas on to the pitch in their purple-striped kit. Tim could hardly hear himself think.

'Jimminy Christmas,' shouted Cairo over the din. 'It's so loud . . . look at Motorway, she loves it.'

Motorway was in her element. She pranced across the lush green turf, acknowledging the crowd on all

sides of the ground, and took her position in the net.

'The llamas seem to be OK with the noise too,' hollered Tim. 'The back four are nearly asleep.'

'They are true pros,' said Cairo proudly.

'I think they'll get a game today, laddies,' said McCloud. 'This will be a real test – a proper team, proper footballers.'

It was a sea of blue in all four stands, apart from one tiny patch of purple, where the Llama United supporters sat. Yes, Llama United now had a few hardcore away supporters who had managed to get tickets for the game. This was especially hard because Llama United didn't have a ticket office. Unsurprisingly, Frank had no idea how to run an actual football club, so all the important jobs that are usually done behind the scenes weren't being done. Don't ask me what these important jobs are – I have no idea. Anyway, back to the supporters. So few, I've actually got time to name them all.

Alongside Molly, Beetroot, Monica and Fiona, who made sure they were at every match wearing embarrassing stripy face paint, there was Pete and his son, Tiny Pete. They lived next door to the White Horse Stadium and were regulars at matches; however, watching a team that actually won games was a huge novelty for them. Tiny Pete had made himself a really good Llama United flag that said: 'C'MON YOU LLAMAS!' This would be impressive if Tiny Pete was between the ages of five and fifteen, but Tiny Pete was thirty-seven. To be honest the flag was a bit wonky. Don't tell Tiny Pete though; he would get ever so upset if he knew I'd been blabbing about it behind his back.

Next came Steve, Kev and Warren, who I can only describe as three idiots. The kind of idiots you see at most football grounds. They all had the same haircut and wore the same clothes. Their language was disgraceful and not something I can repeat here.

Finally, there was Tracey – a short woman who wore the same light-blue anorak wherever she went, whether it was the middle of summer or deepest winter. She had large glasses and long ear lobes that nearly touched her shoulders. Tracey also always wore a greasy red baseball cap that said 'Sea Leopards' across the front of it. I can only assume this is a very small American sports team of some kind.

So that's Llama United's current group of travelling supporters. Five men and five women who had to put up with loads of abuse from the Pirtsmouth fans before the game had even started. Unsurprisingly, only Steve, Kev and Warren fired back with a volley of rude words while Beetroot covered Fiona's ears, and Molly, Monica, Tracey, Pete and Tiny Pete tried to ignore it by reading the programme.

The abuse from the Pirtsmouth fans didn't last for long after kick-off. They went totally silent when, in the first two minutes, Llama United scored! It was a beautiful move. Dasher dribbled round three Pirtsmouth players, then lifted a delightful chip down the wing to the onrushing Cruncher, who whacked in a first time cross to the Duke. He swivelled and nodded the ball towards Goal Machine, who thrashed the ball into the back of the net from six yards out. The keeper was rooted to the spot. Liquid football!

'U–NI–TED, U–NI–TED, U–NI–TED,' came a soft chant from the ten Llama United fans. You'd think they would have come up with something more original by now, although to be fair the word 'llama' is quite hard to work into a good football song.

Tim and Cairo did a two–handed high–five. They'd been doing this after every goal since the second match and it had now become a ritual. However, with all the goals Llama United had scored it was starting to hurt.

The Pirtsmouth captain stormed across to his defence and keeper and shouted at all of them, pointing at various areas of the pitch where he believed they should have been able to stop that attack. It seemed to do the trick, as Pirtsmouth were much improved after they had conceded so early. They had several useful attempts on the Llama United goal, but Ludo was equal to all of them. However, the llamas were not used to a team actually having some shots at goal, and it seemed to spook them a little.

At half-time the score was just 1 – 0. As usual, Tim and Cairo went out on to the pitch to feed and water

the llamas. Tim patted a few of them on the neck and offered them some soft encouraging words, especially to the defence; this was new territory for them.

'It's OK, Bob. You've got the measure of the winger, you can handle him. Stay strong out there, Brian, like a rock. Head up.'

He left his final words for Ludo, who stopped his grass munching and gave Tim a steely glare.

'Good job, Ludo. There will be more shots coming. Do your best. Keep that ball away from Motorway,' he whispered in his ear. Ludo responded with his customary tiny nod. Did Ludo really understand him?

No, he didn't – he's a llama.

Unlike Tim, McCloud seemed to be unhappy with the llamas efforts so far. He stomped across the pitch with his arms folded, which looked really odd.

'Wha' you doing out there, Cruncher?' he bellowed at Smasher. He always struggled to tell which one was which. They were both white, although Cruncher's black nose flash should have made them impossible to mix up. 'Their midfielder is all over you like a cheap suit; you've got to dominate the space, don't let him have an inch.'

He moved on to Brian, who was cleaning his teeth with his tongue. 'Wha' you doing out there, sonny?

Their striker is all over you like a cheap suit; you've got to dominate the space.'

Then he moved on to the Duke, who refused to look McCloud or anyone else in the eye, because he thought he was so posh. 'Wha' you doing out there, sonny?' he yelled. 'Their defender is all over you like a cheap suit; you've got to dominate the space.'

I never said his team talks were inspiring, did I? He went round the rest of the team saying pretty much the same thing, occasionally punching his fist into the palm of his other hand to really ram home the point. It was hard to tell if the llamas were actually listening to him or understood a word he was saying; they just displayed the same nonchalant and slightly arrogant look as always.

The second half kicked off in the same fashion as the last had finished, with Pirtsmouth dominating the play and doing all the attacking. Then, in the fifty-seventh minute, the unthinkable happened; one of the Pirtsmouth strikers headed a fairly ordinary corner into the net and wheeled away to celebrate his equalizer. What the referee hadn't seen was the striker barging into Ludo to get him out of the way as the corner came in. Ludo looked surprised that such a thing had happened.

151

McCloud had seen it though and flew out of the dugout to begin shouting at the fourth official on the side of the pitch. But the goal stood. It was the first time Llama United had let in a goal. They didn't really know what to do with themselves.

Tim dashed out to the side of the pitch and shouted encouragement to the llamas closest to him. He tried to ignore the horrible heavy feeling in his stomach.

'Come on Lightning, come on Smasher, you can do it. Get the ball to Goal Machine. We can still win this!'

Cairo stood beside Tim, waving his hands about and pointing. He had no idea what he was actually doing, but he'd just seen other coaches do it and it looked professional.

The pair of llamas seemed to take Tim's instructions a little too literally. Every time they got the ball they would ping huge, long passes to Goal Machine. Sadly, they were either miscontrolled by Goal Machine or over-hit. It was beginning to look like the match was going to go to a replay at the White Horse Stadium a week on Tuesday, which would be a night game. The White Horse Stadium didn't have floodlights, which would certainly make it interesting.

Then, with two minutes to go, Lightning finally got her long range passing to click. Standing on the edge of the centre circle, she walloped a massive long ball over the entire Pirtsmouth midfield and defence. It looked as though the Pirtsmouth keeper was going to come out and comfortably gather it, but Goal Machine nipped in front and delicately diverted the pass around him, and the ball trickled into the corner of the net. 2 – 1! It wasn't pretty, but they all count.

The baying Pirtsmouth crowd was silenced for the second time, and once again the feeble chanting of 'U–NI–TED, U–NI–TED, U–NI–TED!' could be heard from the ten Llama United fans.

Tim and Cairo forgot their high-five – they were too busy hugging and jumping up and down.

Pirtsmouth frantically pushed forward in the final moments of the game but it wasn't enough. Llama United held on and booked their place in the second round.

The Pirtsmouth fans were not happy; they threw seats, burgers, plastic drinks bottles, tickets and programmes at their players as they left the pitch. Going out of the Cup in the first round was bad, but losing to a team of llamas was unforgivable.

Tim, Cairo, McCloud and Frank got the llamas

and themselves out of the ground as quickly as possible. They didn't want to experience the wrath of the angry Pirtsmouth fans either. Just as they were speeding out of the stadium gates, a huge man dressed in a Pirtsmouth top and covered from head to foot in tattoos stepped out in front of the van. Frank slammed on the brakes. The man started rummaging around his clothing.

'Just drive at him, scare him off!' yelled McCloud. 'He's got a gun in there or something.'

'It's a rocket launcher,' shouted Cairo.

'Quick, Dad, think of something, we've got to get out of here,' cried Tim.

As Frank revved the engine the man pulled off his top to reveal a 'Llama United Forever' T-shirt. He then proudly raised two thumbs and stepped aside to let the van leave.

Llama United were not only winning matches, they were starting to win friends as well.

23

KICKED OUT!

Tim and Frank were sitting in the kitchen having some breakfast the following Saturday morning when there was a loud knock at the door. It was McCloud, but his face was bright red and his lips were pursed so tightly you could hardly see them. He was waving a piece of paper in his hand as he marched into the kitchen.

'Look at this! It's a disgrace, a joke, an absolute farce!' He threw the paper down on the kitchen table.

Tim picked it up and began to read out loud. The letter was on the Cup governing body's headed notepaper and felt thick and expensive to the touch.

Dear Sirs,

After Llama United's first round Cup match on Saturday 20 November against Pirtsmouth FC, a complaint was lodged by the aforementioned club raising concerns as to the contravention of law four in the Rules of the Game.

We have reviewed the complaint
and decided to uphold it. Therefore
Llama United is disqualified from
further participation in this year's
competition.

We do hope this letter finds you in
good spirits.

Cheerio,
The Governing Body

The Governing Body was a really friendly place to work. They did a bit of looking after football in the morning, and then, after a big lunch, they'd sit down and talk about cakes until it was time to go home.

Tim could feel himself trembling with rage as he read. 'What the . . . they can't do that, can they?'

'It looks like they can, laddie,' said McCloud miserably.

Frank grabbed the letter from his son. 'What is law four anyway?'

McCloud grimaced again. 'I looked it up, and it's something to do with players' equipment.'

Tim shook his head furiously; he wasn't ready to give in. 'That doesn't make sense. There's nothing wrong with our equipment.'

'My guess is that they've complained because the llamas don't wear a full kit. They only wear a shirt –

nae shorts, socks or boots,' replied McCloud.

'That's so unfair,' cried Tim. 'What kind of football team goes and moans at the governing body to get us kicked out of the Cup, just because they lost . . . what spoilsports!'

'That's professional football for you, son; naebady wants to lose to a team of llamas, do they? This is an easy way for them to get back in the competition and stop looking so stupid.'

'Can't we challenge the decision?' said Frank to McCloud. 'We can only keep the farm running if we are still in the Cup.'

'Aye, I'm sure we can, but that could take ages and would cost a load of money with lawyers and all that. The second round is in only three weeks' time.'

'This is a nightmare! We haven't got the money for that, or for anything, to be honest,' said Frank, slumping back into his chair.

Tim couldn't hold back his frustration any longer. 'We have to fight this,' he said, banging his fist on the table.

'But how, laddie?' asked McCloud, slumping down into a chair opposite the one Frank was slumping in.

'I don't know,' replied Tim, staring at the floor in despair.

'Ahem, ahem,' said a voice in the doorway. It was Monica, again, holding her laptop.

'You know all the Llama United fans around the world won't stand for this.'

'We've only got a handful of fans. There were only ten at the last match, and four of them were you, your mum, your sister and Molly,' said Frank miserably.

'That's just because we haven't worked out how to sell tickets properly yet,' replied Monica. 'What about all the fans that look at our website? We've got tonnes of them. We'll get a social media campaign going that will make the Governing Body change its mind. I can get it set up this afternoon.'

So, with no help whatsoever from Frank or McCloud, that's exactly what Monica did. However, the internet wasn't working on Saturday, so she had to wait until Sunday afternoon to get it all ready. I could say Tim helped her, but all he did was make 'Mmm, not bad' and 'I like that' noises, which added very little. Oh yes, Cairo also came round, but he was no use whatsoever.

24
SAVE LLAMA UNITED

This bit could have been really boring, including reams of tedious stuff about social media strategy, gaining followers and hashtags . . . but luckily I fell asleep watching Monica at work, so I think it would be best to just skip through it.

'I think we are nearly ready to launch this,' said Monica, putting the finishing touches to a fantastic picture of Tim and Cairo giving Ludo a big hug.

Monica and Tim had hardly moved from the screen for the last five hours, while Cairo was on his four-hundredth spin of the swivel chair he was sitting on and his sixth carton of blackcurrant juice. See, I told you he was no help whatsoever.

'Wow, it looks amazing!' said Cairo when he eventually came to a dizzy halt from his mega spin.

'We just need loads of people to follow us and share

our story and hopefully something will happen,' said Monica.

'Something like . . . we'll get put back in the Cup?' asked Tim.

'I hope so. This will help, but it might not be enough. It could be a long, long battle.'

Monica started furiously typing and then pressed a large blue PUBLISH button. 'That's it, cross fingers time,' she said.

Tim and Cairo's, I mean *Monica's*, 'Save Llama United' social media accounts were a huge hit. In under an hour they had over 50,000 followers who were willing to help the llamas get back in the Cup. Unfortunately for the Governing Body, this meant over half of those followers started firing off angry tweets and comments to the organization. However, there were also a load of positive messages. One in particular caught Monica's eye.

'Oh WOW!' she exclaimed, flinging her arms in the air. 'OH WOW!'

'What is it?' asked Tim, frantically scanning the screen.

Monica pointed at the message with a trembling finger.

'Hey, hey, big luv for my llamas. C'mon you guys –

let them back in!' said the message. It had a picture of a very glossy-looking woman and the name 'Willow Whifflebum' alongside it.

'Who the broken auntie is Willow Whifflebum?' asked Tim.

Monica looked at Tim like he'd just asked the most stupid question ever. 'Really? REALLY? *Everyone* knows who Willow Whifflebum is. Have you been living under a rock?'

'I don't know who she is either,' added Cairo, giving his hand an awkward little shake.

Monica let out a little sigh and then went on a ten-minute ramble about Willow Whifflebum and how great, famous and powerful she was. Tim and Cairo struggled to keep up.

'So basically this Whifflebum person is mega famous, but nobody is really sure why, as she doesn't have a skill,' concluded Tim, when Monica had finished.

'Apart from looking fabulous,' said Monica.

'Is that a skill?' asked Tim.

'Remember though, Tim,' added Cairo, a chuckle in his voice. 'She also married a famous American rapper recently – Two Jackets.'

'You mean Five Jackets,' said Monica. 'The

best rapper in the world.'

As you are already aware, I know very little about hip-hop or these rappers. However, I am aware that Five Jackets is called Five Jackets because he wears five jackets when he is onstage. Yes, it's that unimaginative. Performing under those big stadium lights while wearing all those jackets obviously makes him very hot, sweaty and tired. He usually passes out after just three songs. For some reason this has made him incredibly popular.

Just then another message flashed up on Monica's screen.

'5JKTS, in leather & an anorak 2night. Llamas rule! GovBody – put them back in the Cup – VIP tickets to my gig Sat & after-party with me and my lady. Peace.'

Monica screamed. 'Five Jackets. Five Jackets . . . on my laptop!'

'I think this is a good thing,' said Tim slowly. And it was.

Five Jackets' promise of VIP tickets and an after-party with him and Willow Whifflebum was enough to make the Governing Body have a major rethink. They, like everyone else apart from Tim and Cairo, were huge fans and the tickets were like gold dust.

On Tuesday, the governing body issued a statement to the media.

- - - - *Press Release* - - - -

After a great deal of consideration the Governing Body has decided to reinstate Llama United into this season's Cup competition. We wish them every success in further rounds. Now can everyone please leave us alone because we've got a really big party to get ready for.

Cheerio,
The Governing Body

Tim heard the news as he was getting ready for school. He punched the air and charged downstairs to tell his dad and McCloud, who had been pacing around the kitchen pretty much non-stop since Saturday afternoon. That's a lot of pacing.

'We've done it!' Tim shouted as he leaped into the room.

'You've got all the social media stuff ready?' asked Frank.

'We did all that on Sunday. Haven't you been listening to the news? We are back in the Cup, the Governing Body had a major rethink.'

'Really, it's all over . . . already?' said Frank.

'Yep, we are back in the Cup and get to play Looton Town in the second round in a few weeks.' Tim puffed his chest out proudly as though he'd just climbed a huge mountain.

'Yeeeeeeerrrrhoooooooooooo,' shouted McCloud as he ran over to give Tim a huge hug, followed by a high five, followed by a strange little Scottish dance.

'That's fantastic,' said Frank, a grin breaking out on his face. 'But how did you do it so quickly?'

'It's all incredibly boring, Dad. All you need to know is that we are playing again and some really nice people even donated a bit of money to pay for llama food.'

'Really?' said Frank. He put his hand over his mouth in surprise.

'Yep, people want to see us do well . . . we've got some really nice fans. It's not loads of money, just enough for a few weeks or so.'

Tim saw his dad wipe away a tiny tear as he walked over to give his son a huge hug. Tim felt a bit embarrassed; his dad had never hugged him like this before. Uh oh, was he sobbing on Tim's shoulder? Could have been; I'm not really sure. I'm wondering what it would be like to have a go on Cairo's swivel chair. WEEEEEEEEEEEEEEEeeeeeeeeeee!

'Right then, stop all that soppy stuff,' snapped McCloud. 'We've got llamas to train . . . I want to show them how to do a magic zig-zag one–two–three turn today.'

'Cor, what's that?' asked Tim.

'I've no idea,' said McCloud with a huge grin. 'But it sounds really good doesn't it?'

MATCH REPORT
THE CUP SECOND ROUND:
LOOTON TOWN 0 – 3 LLAMA UNITED

By Steve Buffalo-Mozzarella,
Chief Sports Reporter, Daily Megalomaniac

Looton Town were the latest side to be pulled apart by the rampaging Llama United in the Cup, succumbing to a 3 – 0 defeat at Kenny Road.

Following a late reinstatement into the competition, the Llamas were just too hot to handle, and if it wasn't for the sterling efforts of Looton keeper Sid Kawalski the score could have easily hit double figures.

United's dangerous striker, the Duke, opened the scoring in the fifteenth minute, nodding home a Dasher cross from six yards out. Llama United doubled the score ten minutes later as Goal Machine capitalized on a defensive mix-up in the Looton area to stab home from three yards. The llamas completed the victory with a beautiful twenty-yard lob from Cruncher, after some good work from Lightning on the left wing.

Looton had few chances to get themselves on the score sheet due to an excellent defence marshalled by the towering Brian, their best effort coming from Pete Murray, who ballooned a good ball over the bar from ten yards out. Many believe Murray was scared by the advancing Llama United keeper, Ludo, who once again was in dominant form between the sticks.

After the game, Llama United assistant manager Tim Gravy was thrilled by his team's performance: 'I'm thrilled by our performance today. This could have been a tricky game after what we went through with the Governing Body, but the lads did a great job out there.

'It probably helped that the Llamas knew nothing about being kicked out of the Cup – they just like to focus on their game at all times.'

When quizzed on how far he thought the llamas could go in the competition, Gravy was equally enthusiastic: 'I think we have a great chance of going all the way,' he told reporters.'The team is focused and determined to get the job done. I don't mind who we get in the third round, but it would be great to get one of the really big teams like Munchester United.'

It is still to be confirmed how the llamas gained their football skills. Claims that they are a rare breed from high in the Andes are yet to be authenticated, as our team of reporters went missing in Bolivia two weeks ago.

25
THE THIRD-ROUND DRAW

Any football fan worth their salt knows that the third round Cup draw is one of the most important days in the football calendar. It's when the big boys from the top two leagues join the competition for the first time. For the owners of a smaller club, playing a big one can generate money that they can invest back into the team or help save their club from financial ruin. Frank had slightly more modest dreams – he just wanted to get enough money to keep the farm running for a few more weeks, hopefully even months. He even had a nice fresh page ready in his little black notepad.

Tim, Cairo, Frank and McCloud were at home for the draw, huddled around the TV waiting for the balls to be drawn by an ex-footballer and an actor from a long-running soap opera.

Tim could feel the adrenalin pumping around his body. His palms were sweaty and he nervously paced about the room as the balls were dropped into the swirly container from a velvet bag. Cairo, McCloud and Frank were also pacing about the lounge, and as it wasn't the biggest of rooms, they started bumping into each other. It didn't help anyone's nerves.

'What ball number are we?' asked Cairo for the fifteenth time, gnawing at his nails.

'Number four,' replied Tim, for the fifteenth time.

The ex-footballer was mixing the wooden balls up in the swirly container before he selected the first one.

'Number three,' he said, holding the wooden ball with white writing towards the camera.

'Number three is Beverton, and they will play . . .' came the voice of the main presenter from off screen.

'Ohhh, number three,' howled Cairo. 'That was nearly us.'

'Sssshh,' said Tim.

The actor was now swirling the balls. 'Number five,' he said.

'Number five is East Ham United!' said the main presenter.

'Number five,' wailed Cairo. 'That was nearly us.'

'Ssssh,' said Tim again.

'Number fifteen,' said the ex-footballer.

'Number fifteen is Munchester United.'

'Ohh! Number fifteen. That was nearly us,' howled Cairo again.

'Just be quiet, will you!' hissed Tim. 'Hang on, that's not even close to us.'

'Number twenty-three,' said the actor.

'Number twenty-three is Brustol Town.'

'Awww. I wanted us to play Munchester United,' moaned Tim.

The draw went on for another few minutes and still the number-four ball hadn't been drawn. The actor and the ex-footballer were getting down to the final few balls in the container.

Tim's heart was pumping so fast he could feel it banging against his ribs. 'Got to be careful here,' he said. 'There's still a team left we want to avoid. They've got that massive striker, Elbows McGinty.'

'Number thirty-seven,' said the ex-footballer.

'Number thirty-seven is Borwich City, and they play . . .'

'Number four,' said the actor.

'That's our friends Llama United,' said the presenter with a chuckle. 'Away from home for them. I wonder how they'll get on with Elbows McGinty?'

Tim put his head in hands. Of all the sixty-three

teams they could have drawn, Borwich City was the one they really didn't want. They weren't big enough to give Llama United loads of money, it was a long drive to their ground and they had one of the deadliest strikers in the game – Elbows McGinty. Lethal in front of goal and lethal against the other players. He had already been sent off seven times this season. It should have been about twenty, but most of the referees in the league were scared of him. McGinty made sharks look cuddly.

The Cup was going to become very real for Llama United in early January.

26
ELBOWS IN BORWICH

By the time the third round of the Cup rolled into view, the Gravy farm had been covered in a few feet of snow several times. Despite the bad weather, McCloud carried on his training. He was out doing free-kick training on Christmas morning, corners on Boxing Day evening, and diving headers on New Year's Day. He hardly took a break and didn't seem to spend any time with family or friends. McCloud said his family all lived in Australia and he didn't have the time to visit. This was a lie; they actually lived in New Zealand. McCloud was terrible at geography.

Borwich City's ground was the biggest Tim had been to so far. It held about twenty-eight thousand people, and every seat was either yellow or green. But he wasn't admiring the ground this time – he was on the lookout for Elbows McGinty, the Welsh international who would be returning from a

five-game ban for headbutting.

His first name wasn't really Elbows; it was Trevor. But everyone called him Elbows because he jumped for every high ball with a leading elbow, which would usually catch the poor opposing player going for the ball in the face. Elbows claimed he couldn't help it and even agreed to go for some tests to try and solve the problem. They didn't help. During an international friendly in Peru, the Peruvian goalkeeper was trying to catch a high corner when he had his eyeball poked out by a flailing McGinty elbow. That goalkeeper is now called Patch Sanchez.

When Tim first clapped eyes on Elbows McGinty he was standing in the tunnel just outside the changing rooms. He was scratching the top of his nose. Not the kind of scratch most people do when they scratch their nose (you know, a quick one); he was really scratching it. Tim thought he'd scratch his nose right off he was doing it so hard.

McGinty was a giant of a man, bigger than anyone Tim had ever seen before. He had legs that looked like huge tree trunks that had been pumped full of lead, and a chin that could smash a rock into little tiny pieces. On top of his head was an over-elaborate footballer's haircut. Shaved one side, long on the other, with a ponytail that was pulled into a Mohawk.

Tim was feeling brave, so went over to McGinty and stuck out his hand for a milkshake . . . sorry, I mean handshake. Even I'm nervous.

'Good luck,' said Tim, his voice trembling. 'Have a great game today . . . but hopefully not that great.'

McGinty looked down at Tim from his great height, and then slowly looked at Tim's outstretched hand. Then he slapped it away with one of his huge mitts. WHACK. Ouch! That really hurt. What a horrible man, thought Tim.

Elbows yawned and then carried on scratching his nose, while staring blankly into the distance. Tim stood there awkwardly for a few seconds, his hand throbbing from the wallop it had just received. Then he shuffled away and out of the tunnel. He hated Elbows McGinty even more now.

Cairo was standing by the dugout when he saw Tim trying to rub the pain out of his hand.

'You OK, gaffer?' he asked. Cairo had taken to calling Tim 'gaffer' for some reason.

'That Elbows McGinty,' Tim said through gritted teeth. 'He's just whacked my hand! I was only trying to be nice.'

'That's professional footballers for you,' said Cairo knowledgeably. 'He must have had his game face on.'

'Do you even know what a game face, is Cairo?' asked Tim.

Cairo shrugged. 'I've absolutely no idea.'

Llama United felt the full power of Elbows McGinty in the first five minutes of the match. He launched himself at Bill as a Borwich corner was floated into the area, catching him square on his long hairy chin. Bill staggered back and sank to his knees with a loud yelp; the llama had never been smashed in the face like that before. Ludo immediately stepped between McGinty and poor old Bill and puffed out his chest. As McGinty laughed in the big black llama's face, a

176

few other llamas and Borwich players joined in the pushing and shoving before the referee jumped into the melee, blowing his whistle over and over again.

The Borwich players, who were very experienced in this kind of fracas, backed away and slunk back to their positions before the ref could work out who had been doing the pushing and shoving. The llamas didn't really understand what was going on. It wasn't something that McCloud had practised with them. So they carried on trying to bump the Borwich players, and by mistake the ref. The referee wasn't best pleased with this and showed yellow cards to Ludo, Cruncher and Brian. Then he also gave a yellow to Cairo, who had sprinted on to the pitch with his physio bag to help Bill, because the ref hadn't given him permission to come on.

When the game got started again, Llama United were really spooked by the trouble and didn't seem to be concentrating on the game. Borwich were having a field day and had loads of shots on goal. Luckily for Llama United, Ludo was at the top of his game.

However, with three minutes to go in the first half, Borwich City had the ball in the back of the net and it was Elbows McGinty – who else? McGinty collected the ball about twenty yards out and charged straight at Bill who, unusually, stepped aside straight away; he didn't want to get hit again. Elbows then dribbled round Brian . . . twice, which is quite a rare skill for such a big lumbering striker to perform. Once inside the area he unleashed an unstoppable drive into the top right-hand corner of the net. Ludo didn't stand a chance . . . it was, after all, *unstoppable*. I don't use that word lightly.

The final cherry on the top for McGinty was when the ball went on to hit Motorway square on the side of the body, causing her to let out a loud and painful bleat.

Borwich City 1 – 0 Llama United.

Tim threw the water bottle he was holding to the ground in frustration. Cairo was desperate to charge on and check on Motorway, but Tim held him back. He didn't want his friend to get another yellow. Cairo sat and fumed. He didn't like having to wait for the ref's instructions to come on and give medical attention to his team.

McGinty, ever the one to revel in his goal celebrations, ran around the llamas as though he was riding an imaginary horse, then made a boo-hoo gesture to Bill, who looked totally confused. Elbows then completed the routine with a frankly disgusting 'milking the cow' mime. He clearly had no idea what kind of animal he was playing against.

When the llamas got back to the changing room it wasn't a happy place. Especially as nobody had cleaned away the llama poo from before the game. Tim wondered if it would have been better if they'd stayed on the pitch.

McCloud was pacing aggressively up and down as they all filed in, muttering under his breath.

'Sit down,' he barked. Then he realized that none of the llamas could sit down on chairs; instead they just stood there looking at him blankly.

'What the hell was that?' he continued to bark. 'That was a disgrace. That's the worst I've ever seen you play. You just gave up and let that thug Elbows McGinty take control. He's laughing at you out there. Don't you want to wipe that smile off his face in the second half?'

The llamas stared back at McCloud. Tim could see Ludo's long neck slump forward slightly, like it had the first day he'd met him. He clearly wasn't happy.

'Second half, get out and give them a taste of their own medicine – get tough,' shouted McCloud, then he went over to Bill and went right up to his furry

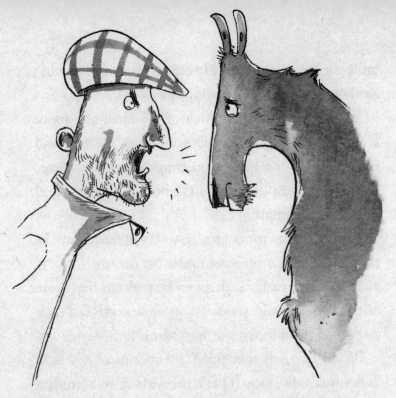

face. 'And you, you cannae let him do that. You are a huge llama; you shouldn't be taking that from him – he thinks you are weak! Get a grip. If we don't score we are out!' Then he stormed out, slamming the door behind him. Well, he tried to slam the door, but it was a safety door so it had one of those soft-close mechanisms.

Bill looked sad. He had always been considered one of the toughest of the four defenders, but that smash in the face had rocked him to his very core. His chin was still fizzing in pain; what it needed was a nice packet of frozen peas. But being a llama he couldn't ask for the peas and, perhaps more importantly, didn't actually know what peas were. So he just continued to look sad.

Tim didn't like the shouty approach of McCloud or seeing the llamas upset. He preferred soft words of encouragement. When he got to Bill on his water round, the poor llama was looking sadder than ever. 'C'mon Bill, you can do it,' Tim whispered softly in the llama's ear. 'I know you're a great player. Show McGinty no fear; get him with a few tackles early doors. Give him a scare; show him how tough you really are.'

Tim wasn't sure if this had worked, but Bill had raised his neck and was holding his head high again. Out of the corner of his eye, Ludo gave him one of his little nods. On the other side of the changing room Bob looked in the mirror at his brilliant hair . . . again! He hadn't listened to any of the team talk.

Bill certainly did get a few tackles in 'early doors' as requested, sending Borwich players flying left, right and centre. One was so hard the right winger crashed into the advertising hoardings on the side of the pitch and lay on the turf for a good few minutes,

181

softly calling 'Mummy, Mummy!'

However, after his early success Bill did get a little carried away. Sixty minutes in he mistimed a tackle just inside the area and Borwich were awarded a penalty. It was also a yellow card for Bill. Even worse was that McGinty was Borwich's penalty taker, and he hadn't missed a penalty in five years. Tim felt guilty that he'd given Bill the wrong instructions. McCloud started wailing at the top of his voice.

As McGinty carefully placed the ball on the penalty spot, Ludo wandered off his line to go and look at him. Nothing really unusual there; lots of goalkeepers do this to penalty takers to psych them out.

OK, this was slightly unusual, as the goalkeeper in question was a llama.

'Get away from me you dirty bag of fur,' snarled McGinty as he went eye to eye with Ludo.

Ludo nodded at McGinty and suddenly fired a tiny squirt of spit from the corner of his mouth. It was amazingly accurate and went straight into McGinty's left eye. Then Ludo casually returned to his position in goal.

'What was that?' screamed Elbows McGinty, wiping his eye. 'Did you see that ref? That flaming cow donkey thing spat in me eye!'

'Just take the penalty, McGinty,' shouted the ref. 'I haven't got time for any of your tricks today. I just want this game over as quickly as possible. I'm worried about all the llama poo on the pitch.'

'But he spat in my eye,' moaned McGinty, rubbing his eye with the grubby corner of his shirt. 'You've got to send him off.'

'I didn't see it, McGinty, and if you don't get on

and take the penalty I'll have to book you for time-wasting.'

McGinty muttered under his breath and got ready to take the penalty. He'd rubbed most of the horrible llama spit out of his eye, but his vision wasn't as clear as it normally was. He marked out his trademark long penalty run-up, ready to blast the ball into the top corner as he usually did. It was such a formality some of the Borwich fans didn't even bother to watch.

But as he commenced his run-up, his eye started itching horrendously and it totally put him off. He still blasted the ball, but this time it went high, wide and handsome into the fans behind the goal, smashing someone's mobile phone out of their hand. They really should have been watching the pitch.

The crowd went totally silent. Apart from the small cluster of purple-striped Llama United fans at the other end of the ground. Their numbers had swelled to over two hundred now, so obviously I can't name them all this time. Their songs hadn't got any better though.

'U-NI-TED, U-NI-TED, U-NI-TED,' was still all they could muster.

In the dugout Tim, Cairo and McCloud briefly celebrated the miss, but then quickly charged to the side of the pitch to shout instructions; they still had to get back into this match.

With the penalty miss and McGinty still struggling with his sore eye, Borwich City seemed to lose their attacking focus and appeared to be happy sitting back and settling for a 1 – 0 win. McGinty spent all his time rubbing at his eye with his shirt and fingers – which if anything was making things worse. He poured water into the now bloodshot eye and even had the physio on twice to check it, but he couldn't find anything wrong. McGinty was so distracted that he hardly touched the ball for the rest of the match.

Llama United, however, finally found their feet. With twenty minutes to go Cruncher brought the score level with a superb piledriver from twenty-five yards out. Not a keeper in the world could have stopped it. Tom and Cairo leaped from the dugout and knee-slid across the technical area turf in wild celebration. In the stands Frank, Beetroot, Monica and Molly leaped up and down with the rest of the llama fans. Fiona remained seated – she was listening to Five Jackets' latest song – 'My Zip is Stuck' – on her phone.

Then, with just two minutes left, a Borwich defender fouled Lightning just outside the area. It's quite easy to foul a llama to be honest; they have four legs to tackle, so chances are you are going to smack into one of them. This free kick was the perfect range for Dasher, who McCloud had been paying special attention during dead-ball training on Christmas morning. Borwich had everyone back in the area and had built a six-man wall, which included the huge McGinty, still rubbing his eye.

Dasher took a three-step run-up and curled the ball up and over the wall, aiming for the top corner of the net. But the keeper had spotted the plan and was moving across to the corner of the goal to make the save. Tim put his hands over his eyes, leaving a tiny crack to watch through. Just as the ball cleared the wall it took a deflection off McGinty's elbow, which was up at a right angle as he rubbed his eye. The ball ricocheted in the opposite direction to where the keeper was going and looped into the other side of the net.

Borwich City 1 – 2 Llama United. What drama!

The referee blew the final whistle not long after that. Llama United were through to the fourth round of the Cup! Tim, Cairo and McCloud couldn't quite believe it as they hugged and hopped up and down on the side of the pitch. The llamas just stood there wondering what all the fuss was about.

27
THE BANKING CRISIS

The phone at the Gravys' farmhouse was ringing constantly after the Borwich clash. This was all down to Beetroot and Molly's lovely Llama United scarves. Everyone wanted one. They had only finished six in total because they weren't brilliant at knitting, and they were struggling to keep up with the number of requests. The new Llama United fans also wanted T-shirts, flags, kits and hats, and there was one odd request for a huge papier mâché Goal Machine head, who was easily the ugliest of all the llamas.

The kitchen table was a sea of purple wool, knitting needles and bits of material. Occasionally Monica would offer to help, but she was so snowed under looking after all the social media accounts and the website she just didn't have time. Tim didn't know the first thing about knitting, and Fiona was only keen on trying to balance large balls of wool on her head.

Frank was no help either. When he wasn't doing maths in his little black notepad, he was fiddling around in the first field. He still hadn't finished Fiona's princess castle, which was making her angry, and his beekeeping attempts had gone horribly wrong. He'd risked some of the money they'd earned from the Borwich City match on six beehives and thousands and thousands of bees. However, he forgot to buy any queen bees, so nothing really happened. A few thousand went on holiday and I heard a rumour that a handful opened a cereal cafe somewhere, but that's about it. To make matters worse, Frank's beekeeper costume was very cheap and offered virtually no protection. Every evening he returned to the farmhouse with an interesting array of stings and bumps over his body. When a bee stung him inside his right nostril, he decided it was time to try something less dangerous.

One evening as Frank was serving dinner (he'd taken over cooking duties from the overworked Beetroot), there was a firm knock on the door.

Frank left the burned chicken he was trying to remove from a baking tray to see who was there. He returned a few minutes later with a man in a crisp blue suit, white shirt and a plain dark-blue tie. His face was very solemn, as if he'd never heard a joke in his entire life.

'Sorry to interrupt your evening, everyone,' said the man in an unusually high-pitched voice.

The rest of the Gravy family stopped what they were doing, which was mainly trying to work out how to set the dinner table around a mountain of half-finished Llama United scarves, and stared at the stranger.

'This man is from the bank,' announced Frank. 'He's here to talk about a few money problems we might be having with the farm and what he can do to help.'

The man shifted uneasily in his suit and looked at the ground. Tim knew straight away this man wasn't a goodie.

'I see your team of llamas are doing well in the Cup,' said the man, with zero emotion in his face.

'Yes, they are doing well thanks to my son here,' replied Frank proudly, pointing at Tim. Tim felt hot. He was always embarrassed when he got praise from his dad.

'Well, the bank is taking a keen interest in the team's progress, and have decided that with the all extra money you're receiving from the team's success, we can increase the payments you owe us.'

Frank and Beetroot both opened their mouths, a little shocked by this statement.

'We aren't actually making much money,' replied Frank eventually. 'We've just about got enough to pay you what we currently owe each month with a bit left to live on, but that's it.'

'The bank has concluded that as you gain more supporters you will gain more money from ticket sales and merchandise.' He pointed at the pile of wool and scarves on the kitchen table.

Tim noticed the man couldn't stop sweeping his short, greasy brown hair away from his forehead every time he spoke. After a while this was all Tim could concentrate on, and he began to count the number of times the man did it.

'Llama United has a few hundred supporters who go to the matches, and our merchandising is run by my wife,' said Frank, pointing at Beetroot. 'We won't be able to get you the money you need.'

The man smiled oddly, displaying a small number of gold teeth in the corner of his mouth. Then he touched his hair again. 'I'm afraid if you can't pay the required amount, we'll have to take the farm off you. It's very simple, Mr Gravy.'

Frank put his head in his hands and slumped down in a chair. Tim looked around the kitchen; apart from the man from the bank, everyone was totally glum, even Fiona (but mainly because her dinner had been delayed).

Tim wasn't going to let this nasty man ruin his family. 'You know what, mister bank person?' he said, moving closer to the man and wagging his finger. 'My llamas are going to win the Cup and we'll get enough money to stop you taking the farm away from us.'

'You'd better hurry up then. The clock is ticking,' the bank manager replied coldly.

He placed a piece of paper on the table in front of Frank. 'That's the new amount we need to receive at the end of every month, starting immediately.'

Frank didn't look up.

'Oh and good luck with the Cup. You're playing the team I support in the next round . . . I'll see myself out.' With that he slithered out of the room.

Beetroot and Frank were silent for a few minutes. The colour in their faces had drained away. Frank started thumbing through his little black notepad anxiously.

'Don't worry, I think it's going to be all right,' said Tim enthusiastically. 'We'll play really well in the next few rounds and we are bound to get more supporters and sell more tickets.'

'Plus we'll all chip in with the merch, Mum,' added Monica. 'There's a T-shirt-printing machine at college, which I'm sure we can use.'

'And I'm sure Molly can find some extra volunteers for the animal shelter so she can help you more with the merchandise here,' said Tim. 'Cairo is always saying there are loads of people that want to look after rescue animals. Until they meet the goats . . .'

Frank and Beetroot slowly began to smile. It was great to hear their children try to think of solutions to their money problems.

'You know what, you are both right,' said Frank. 'We can do this if we all pull together! We'll make this a proper farm . . . just one that has llamas who play football and that sells T-shirts and scarves instead of potatoes and carrots.

This was the first time in ages that Tim had seen his dad really energized.

'I'm also going to give up beekeeping and start

making wine,' he announced boldly. Beetroot and Monica rolled their eyes.

'I can also help,' announced Fiona at the top of her voice. 'By eating my dinner . . . that is now four hours late.'

The burned chicken was chucked away and dinner became beans on toast, if you're interested. Nasty cheap beans. And the toast? Brown wholemeal; the most boring type of bread. I think I'd rather have what the llamas were having.

28

BULTON ATHLETIC V
LLAMA UNITED

The fourth round was another away match against a team called Bulton Athletic, who last season had been relegated from the top division. All their best players had been sold and they'd been left with a team full of young players desperately trying to make a name for themselves. Their manager, Ted Peters, was also young and fairly inexperienced. He looked like a baby in an expensive suit.

When the two teams were led out on to the pitch, Tim noticed that Peters was escorting a tiny, cute black lamb by a blue piece of string. He was grinning from ear to ear and trying to catch Tim's attention.

'Ha ha, look what I've got,' he called to Tim, nodding at the lamb. 'We've also got a sheep. What you going to do about that?'

'Do about what?' shouted Tim.

'We are going to put this lamb in our goal and

then your llamas won't shoot at it. 'Coz llamas like to protect sheep and lambs, don't they?'

'Where did you find out about that?' replied Tim casually. He was trying to show he wasn't concerned by this sheep tactic, but it made him slightly worried, what if it worked? What if his llamas wouldn't be keen on shooting at the goal with the tiny, cute black lamb in it? They couldn't afford to get knocked out of the Cup now, especially after the visit from the bank manager.

'I read about it. Llamas are programmed to protect things, guard stuff and all that.'

Cairo had noticed the manager and Tim exchanging words across the pitch and had been listening in. 'It's only certain llamas that like to be guards,' he called helpfully. 'Not all of them are like that. Goal Machine doesn't care about what he's shooting at. He's just hungry for goals.' He gave Tim a wink, which made Tim feel instantly better.

Ted Peters' smug face dropped, but he tried to brush off what Cairo had said. 'I don't believe you. Just watch, you'll hardly have a shot on goal, especially as my little lamb is really cute and I've got a really good goalkeeper.'

'We'll see, shall we,' Cairo shouted back.

Ted Peters tied the little black lamb into Bulton's goal, whispered something to his keeper and left the pitch. The lamb did not look happy; the hubbub of the expectant crowd before kick-off was making him nervous. He was also slightly angry nobody had bothered to give him a name.

As the first whistle blew the crowd roared loudly and started singing several boisterous songs. The cute, little black lamb let out a panicked bleat and starting frantically running about the goal. The Bulton keeper, who was trying to concentrate on the game, was distracted by the panicking animal and tried to calm it down. This seemed to make the lamb even more stressed.

At the other end of the pitch Motorway sat in her goal

chewing at the lush green grass around her. She was an experienced pro now and the roar of the crowd had a calming effect on her. Plus, this was some of the best grass she had eaten during the cup run.

'Your little lamb doesn't like the noise of the crowd,' Tim shouted to Ted Peters across the technical area on the side of the pitch.

Peters tried to ignore him and focus on the match, but out of the corner of his eye he could see his keeper chasing the little lamb around his goalmouth. It was like playing with ten men.

As Cairo had predicted, the lamb didn't bother Goal Machine in the slightest. After ten minutes he chipped in his first goal from forty yards out – into what was pretty much an empty net, as the keeper wasn't watching. Goal Machine wheeled away and wiggled his hips in delight, it was the first time Tim had noticed something that resembled a celebration. Goal Machine actually had a few lice and they were making him itch, but Tim wasn't to know that.

Goal Machine's next goal came in the twenty-fifth minute; a low drive from outside the area. The keeper had finally managed to catch the little lamb and was holding it in his arms, so he couldn't go for the ball.

By now, Peters had realized he'd made a huge

mistake and was frantically trying to substitute the little lamb from the field of play. But as the lamb wasn't technically a player or actually on the playing area, being behind the goal line, Peters wasn't allowed to remove it. The fourth official kept instructing him that he could only make the switch at half-time.

The Bulton keeper was now forced to play the rest of the half with a cute little lamb in his arms and had to kick everything away. He was half a keeper.

Llama United's third goal came from a beautiful bit of skill from Dasher on the wing. She turned two Bulton players inside out on the edge of the area, then whacked a rabona into the top right-hand corner of the net. This was at exactly the same time as the cute, little black lamb decided to go to the toilet on the Bulton keeper. He wasn't happy – it was his lucky top.

The lamb didn't appear on the pitch for the second half but it didn't make any difference; Bulton were already beaten. The Duke majestically headed the fourth and fifth goals from corners, and those were the final nails in the Bulton coffin.

Ted Peters didn't shake Tim, McCloud or Cairo's hand after the match – he just stormed off down the tunnel. The Bulton keeper, however, did shake Tim's hand and was polite enough to thank him for the match.

'Why did you shake his hand?' whispered Cairo to Tim after the keeper had left.

'I was just being nice, you know – a proper sportsman.'

Cairo raised his eyebrows. 'He's probably got lamb's wee and poo all over his hands though.'

'UUUURRRRGGGGGHHHHHH!' cried Tim.

29
THE GEOFF COREN SHOW

As any seasoned football fan knows, football can occasionally be very boring. Often you go to matches only to find your mind wandering on to what you should have for dinner or how many plates you could stack on your head before they fall off. Sometimes you'll spend a good chunk of the match watching other people in the crowd to see what they are doing. Look, someone's losing their temper over a throw-in; oh, that chap is going to spill all those drinks . . . oh no he hasn't! Well played, sir. Anything, really, to take your mind off the tedious spectacle that is happening on the rectangular piece of turf in front of you.

For Llama United, the fifth round was very boring. They drew a small league team called Gubbins Town, who had somehow fluked their way into the latter stages of the competition. So compared to facing Borwich City they were a really easy side to play.

Llama United won the match 3 – 0; once again Goal Machine lived up to his name by scoring two, and the Duke got the other with a header. The Duke loved scoring goals. He would arrogantly pose in a defiant manner, holding his head as high as possible towards the rival fans. Which they hated.

McCloud, Tim and Cairo sat in McCloud's office in the corner of the llama barn, listening to the quarter-final draw on the radio. The Scottish manager had started to grow a beard at the start of the Cup, which he was only going to shave off when Llama United had been knocked out of the competition, so it was getting really long and itchy now. Soup and other bits of food had nestled their way into it over the weeks, and several people had pointed out that he probably had enough for a sandwich filling in there if he gave it a really good scratch.

Over in the main field, Frank was busy trying to construct his vineyard, which was going just about as well as the building of Fiona's princess castle; that is to say, terribly. He hadn't realized you first need to build an elaborate fencing structure to hang the grape vines on. It was making him very angry, so he wasn't listening to the draw.

The result was that Llama United were to be pitted against Enfield Hotspurts in the quarter-final of the Cup, away from home again. They were a Premier League team who regularly played in Europe and had a whole host of expensive players and internationals. However, it was the manager that McCloud was worried about. He was a devious, mean-spirited little man with huge white hair. He always appeared to be chewing on gum, but actually it was the inside of his cheek.

The manager's name was Geoff Coren, but he made everyone call him 'Guv' because he saw himself as the ultimate football manager; one who should be respected by all. McCloud knew Geoff Coren would have a trick up his sleeve to deal with Llama United.

Perhaps I should go and see what Geoff Coren is up to? Then *we'll* all know what's going on, even if Tim, Cairo and McCloud won't . . .

Geoff Coren was looking in the huge gold-framed mirror that he'd hung up in his massive lavish office at the Enfield Hotspurts ground. He was brushing his huge mane of white hair, up and back, up and back, up and back, until it reached a height he deemed acceptable. When he'd finished, he smugly admired himself in the mirror. Geoff Coren loved everything about himself, apart from his lack of height. To combat this he made his hair big and wore platform shoes and extra-thick socks. This didn't make a great deal of difference, if I'm honest with you.

Geoff Coren's teams were very successful and made him loads of money. Frank's little black notepad wouldn't have been able to handle the amount of money Geoff Coren shuffled around.

After a full ten minutes of hair brushing, Geoff Coren sat back at

203

his desk and lovingly admired a huge pile of player contracts he had been working on for weeks. Geoff Coren didn't like computers – he wrote everything down using an expensive fountain pen. He rubbed the contracts against the side of his face and took a deep sniff of their inky goodness.

On top of this pile was a brand spanking new contract for his own job. He had spent months lovingly crafting every single aspect of the huge fifty-page document and it was the only version he had drawn-up. It was incredibly boring, but worth so much money that Frank could have bought ten farms with it. Geoff Coren treated it like it was a baby and regularly talked to it in a coochie-coo-coo voice.

'Oooh hello, my little precious darling . . .' he whispered now to his new contract. 'Did you sleep well and gets lots of important rest?' Geoff Coren knew that if he won the Cup this season the owners of the club were bound to sign the document. He certainly didn't want to miss out on millions of pounds by losing to a team of llamas.

On the other side of the desk was a thick file marked 'Llama United'. It held all the information he had on the team gathered by his large network of scouts; scouts are the people who spy on other teams and steal their players and ideas. He leafed through it, stopping when he came to the section marked *Dangerous*. It had one page and it was solely dedicated to Goal Machine.

Goal Machine had become a bit of a star over the course of the competition, helped by a hatful of brilliant goals. He was the main player everyone looked out for and the one most of the other llamas always passed to. If he wasn't so ugly, he could probably have earned loads of money for Frank by doing TV commercials for aftershave and really overpriced cars. But sadly he was just too weird-looking. And a llama.

In bold writing under the picture of Goal Machine were the words 'STOP HIM AND WE'LL WIN THE GAME'.

Geoff Coren rubbed his forehead a few times to get his brain warmed up, and then wrote the words *Goal Machine* at the top of a blank piece of paper and underlined them a few times. Then he started to write in large capitals.

POISON?
KIDNAP?
MURDER?
ASSAULT?

CAREER-THREATENING INJURY?

ACCIDENT?

~~MURDER?~~ (Which he then crossed out, as he'd already written it.)

He stood up and began pacing around his plush office on his double-thickness white carpet that was softer than any bed. Occasionally he would stop to look out of the huge window that overlooked the pitch and catch his own reflection in it, which he would smile at, like the peacock he was. Then he'd return to his paper and cross off one of the words from his list.

He continued this pacing, looking out the window, checking his reflection and crossing out words until he had just one option left:

KIDNAP

Don't ask me how he came to this conclusion. I'm just watching him; I'm not in Geoff Coren's brain. It did make him laugh though, an evil cackling laugh that went on for far too long.

He decided that the best way of doing the kidnap would be on the morning of the match when Tim, Cairo and McCloud were out inspecting the pitch. Nobody would ever think one of the llamas could be kidnapped on the morning of the match. Most people would presume Goal Machine had just

206

wandered off – after all, he was a llama.

All Geoff Coren would have to do would be to sneak into the dressing room, lead Goal Machine away from the team and hide him in his office for the whole match. The crucial bit would be leaving the dressing-room door open, so it would be easy for everyone to assume that the llama had just wandered off. The llamas would then have to play without their star striker and with only ten llamas on the field, so would probably lose. This would be a doddle.

He looked at himself in the mirror again. 'You, Geoff, are a genius,' he said to himself, and then he started brushing his hair again.

Rumour has it ninety per cent of all the best managers in the world talk to themselves in the mirror as they brush their hair. The other ten per cent are bald.

30
THE KIDNAP

Enfield Hotspurts's ground was even more impressive than Borwich City's. It was beautiful, both inside and out. Everything from the main door to the toilets looked expensive. Even the receptionist's teeth sparkled like diamonds.

As Geoff Coren had predicted, Tim, Cairo and McCloud were keen to get out on the pitch before the game to have a look at the surface and soak up the pre-match atmosphere. They left all the llamas in the huge dressing room with some water and extra hay and went down the tunnel and out into cavernous 50,000-seat arena. About 600 of these were filled with Llama United fans. Frank, Monica, Molly, Beetroot and Fiona were settling into their seats high up in the stands. Even though they were part of Llama United's backroom staff they had still had to buy their own tickets, which weren't cheap; yet another cost to be scribbled down in Frank's little black notepad. Enfield Hotspurts weren't giving their rivals any special treatment.

This was Geoff Coren's chance! He quickly snuck into the away dressing room with a huge bag of carrots and starting looking for Goal Machine. Geoff Coren wasn't to know that llamas aren't that fussed about carrots. They much prefer Worcester sauce-flavoured crisps.

The changing room stank of llama poo, and Geoff Coren's nose immediately tried to climb off his face. He pinched his nostrils to stop it escaping and pushed his way into the mass of eleven llamas that were standing in the middle of the room. Now, which one was Goal Machine? From the grainy monochrome picture in Geoff Coren's secret file, Goal Machine was white with a black flash across his nose. He peered at each llama in turn and held the photo up to their faces. It was hard to tell which one was which; the secret photos weren't brilliant. Eventually he arrived at one with a black flash across his nose.

Geoff Coren scooped up the long rope wrapped around the llama's neck and pulled him towards the door. The llama didn't seem to be that bothered about being tugged along and happily followed.

Having made sure all the doors in the dressing room were wide open to make it look like the llama had left of his own accord, Geoff Coren raced the animal along the corridor, into the nearest lift and then up two floors to his office. Once inside the office he emptied a bag of vegetables on the floor, tied the long rope to a heavy gold lampshade he had in one corner of the room and left, locking the door behind him. His plan had worked! He took a quick look at himself in another mirror that was just outside his office, told his reflection he was a 'genius' and scuttled off. The game kicked off in just ten minutes. Nobody would find the llama before then and nobody would ever dare look in a well-respected manager's office.

As Geoff Coren got back into the lift he sang a little song to himself. 'Ooh, Geoff aren't you great. Yes, I'm great. Geoff, Geoff, Geoff. Great, Great, Great.'

Geoff Coren was not very good at making up songs.

31
THE HUNT

The whistle blew and the quarter-final between Enfield Hotspurts and Llama United kicked off to a huge roar from both sets of supporters.

Tim was settling himself down in one of the comfy dugout seats when he noticed Cairo standing on the edge of the technical area, pointing and counting to himself. When he'd finished he turned to the dugout, a flash of panic on his face.

'We've only got ten llamas!' he shouted.

'What?' replied Tim, cupping a hand behind his ear.

'We've only got ten llamas!' Cairo shouted with more urgency over the din of the wild crowd. 'One of them is missing.'

Tim got up and began frantically counting the llamas, which wasn't easy as they were all buzzing about in a blur of purple stripes. But Cairo was right;

there were only ten llamas on the pitch. Tim's tummy flipped.

'We'll have to look for him while the game is on,' said Cairo. 'McCloud will have to manage the team on his own for now.'

'OK,' replied Tim anxiously. 'I'll take the left side of the ground and you take the right side. It's so big – I'm worried we'll never find him!'

'Don't worry,' said Cairo. 'He can't have gone far. It's a big stadium but someone is bound to notice a rather famous, great big llama wandering about and return him to us.'

'What happens if he's escaped outside?'

Cairo shrugged. There was good chance this could have happened, but he didn't want to make Tim panic any more than he was already. 'Nah, they shut all the doors once everyone is inside the stadium. I doubt he'll find a way out,' he lied. 'We'll find him in no time, don't worry.'

Tim and Cairo sprinted into the underbelly of the ground and began hunting for the missing llama. We will follow Tim rather than Cairo, mainly because his mission was a bit more exciting – Cairo just got lost near the toilets.

*

If you have ever been behind the scenes at a football ground you'll know it can be a warren of meeting rooms, corporate boxes, restaurants, bars and conference suites. Big grounds like Enfield Hostpurts's seem to need more of these than anyone else. How many conferences can a football club hold at one time? thought Tim as he charged through another huge room full of empty chairs all looking forlornly at an empty stage. As he searched he could hear the muffled noise of the crowd watching the match, and he could tell it was still 0 – 0 because he hadn't heard any huge roars.

When he reached the second level he was presented with a long corridor of firmly shut doors. He tried the first one on his left, which had the name 'Roberts' stamped on it. The door opened straight away and it was full of people stuffing their faces with food and drink, chatting and laughing. Nobody seemed to be the slightest bit bothered by what was happening on the pitch. A bored-looking waiter, who can't have been much older than Tim, was standing in the corner checking his phone. When he saw Tim he slipped the phone back into his pocket and straightened up.

'Can I help you, sir?' he said to Tim as politely as possible. He had been trained to act like this no matter who he was talking to. Tim could be an important billionaire's son for all he knew . . . dressed in a Llama United tracksuit.

Tim was surprised to be called 'sir' by someone who was probably in the middle of his A Levels. 'Oh, sorry,' he bumbled. 'I was just looking for a missing llama.'

'Aren't they all on the pitch?' asked the waiter.

A tall, thin wiry man in a really bright white suit and red-and-yellow splurgey shirt interrupted the conversation. The man's outfit was so dazzling it made Tim feel a little bit sick, and it took him a while to realize he was being spoken to.

'I said . . . you've only got ten haven't you?' he repeated, chuckling at Tim.

'Yes, you've noticed.'

'Well, to be honest, not really.' The brightly dressed man ushered Tim to the window to show him the pitch. 'Having ten men . . . er, llamas, doesn't seem to be making much difference at all. Hotspurts can hardly get the ball off them.'

As he spoke, one of the llamas – it was hard to tell which one as Tim was so far up – fired a crashing long-range drive at the Hotspurts goal, but unluckily it cannoned off the crossbar and drifted out for a goal kick. Tim instinctively threw his hands up to his head and let out an 'Ooooohhh!' It was mighty close.

'It looks like they're going to score in a minute,' said the man.

Though Tim would have loved to carry on watching through the window, he had to find the missing llama. He was getting hotter and hotter the longer it took.

'Don't worry,' the thin man in the white suit shouted as Tim backed out of the room and carried on up the corridor. 'I'm sure he'll turn up. Good luck!'

Tim tried every door on the left side of the corridor but they were all full of corporate guests eating and drinking and occasionally watching the match. He turned his attention to the doors on the right. There weren't as many of these and nearly all of them were locked, apart from one that was full of brooms and buckets. Tim puffed out his cheeks. He had a nasty feeling in his stomach he wasn't going to find his missing llama here.

He dropped down a few steps into an area that was slightly different from the corporate corridor. These rooms looked like offices. There were three doors labelled 'Coren', 'MacIntosh' and 'Dr Baker'. Dr Baker's was open. It was full of medical kit and a physio table and all sorts of medical bits and bobs; it was the kind of room he could see Cairo in, looking after the llamas after a match. Sadly, there was no llama in here now.

MacIntosh and Geoff Coren's rooms were both locked, although he could hear a great deal of noise coming from Geoff Coren's office, as if someone was wrestling a crocodile. Tim pushed at the handle and barged the door with his shoulder but it wouldn't budge. He tried again, giving it a really big slam this time like the police do in films. But unlike in films, this door remained firm – no eleven-year-old boy was getting past *him*. The door prided himself on his strength, especially because his brother was a much softer touch; he worked at the back of a fried chicken shop that was always getting robbed, mainly because you only had to waggle his handle a few times and he would open.

'Oi, you!' came a loud voice from down the corridor. Tim looked up; there was a heavily built man in a smart black suit, white shirt and thin black tie storming down the corridor towards him. He was wearing shades and had a plastic headset coil coming out of his ear. Tim felt his face go hot and his back go sweaty; he'd been caught in the act.

'Oi!' the bull-headed security guard shouted again as he got closer. Just then, there was a huge roar from the stands above. Someone had scored.

Tim didn't have time to explain what he was doing as the man grabbed him by the collar of his tracksuit and frogmarched him back up to the corporate corridor, down a couple of flights of stairs at the other end and through the large stadium front doors, where he threw Tim unceremoniously to the concrete floor. 'No one is allowed to trespass on football club property, especially not staff offices,' the man shouted at Tim before turning away and going back into the ground.

There was another huge noise from the crowd. Had

someone scored again? Tim was desperate to find out. He picked himself up and rubbed his knees. How was he going to get back in? Then he saw another door that was wide open, a little bit farther down the side of the stadium. Tim dashed through it and followed the corridor on the other side, which led all the way to the away-team dressing room. Oh no, this is how the llama must have escaped!

Just as he was about to head back down the corridor and start searching outside the ground, the dressing-room door swung open and McCloud pranced in with the rest of the hot and sweaty llamas behind him.

'Two-nil, laddie,' he said to Tim with a cheer. 'Goal Machine is on fire today.' He grabbed the llama closest to him and gave it a massive hug. This was Goal Machine. You could tell because he had really wonky bottom teeth jutting out over his top lip and a grey flash across his nose. Yep, that's right – Geoff Coren had kidnapped the wrong llama. The pictures in his secret file were in black and white, making it almost impossible to tell the difference between a black flash across a llama's nose and a grey one! Although Goal Machine's terrible teeth should have been a bit of a giveaway. I wonder when Geoff will work out that he's got things just a teensy bit wrong?

In the Enfield Hotspurts changing room, Geoff Coren was standing perfectly still, inwardly fuming while his coaching staff shouted at his players. Geoff Coren wasn't only fuming at the team, he was fuming at his scouts. Had they put the wrong picture of Goal Machine in his top-secret file, he wondered? If the llama with the black flash across his nose was not Goal Machine, who the blazes was in his office?

Geoff Coren ran upstairs and frantically unlocked his office door. It looked like a bomb had hit it. Imagine ten of the messiest five-year-olds' bedrooms ever, treble it and add five more. Everything was trashed. All his books had been pulled out of the bookshelf, his lampshade was smashed on the floor, his desk and chair were upside down, and all his memorabilia trophies and pictures were dented, broken or smashed. The double-thickness white carpet had mucky llama footprints and bite marks all over it.

Standing in the middle of all this carnage was Cruncher, casually chewing a huge wad of paper. Geoff Coren stared at the llama for a few seconds . . . paper . . . PAPER!

'What's that paper?' he barked at the llama.

Cruncher carried on chewing, turning his head

away from Geoff Coren in disdain. Geoff Coren scampered around his desk hunting for his pile of lovingly handwritten player contracts. Then he noticed with horror that by Cruncher's feet was his own personal contract, the one he spent months and months writing. The only copy he had.

Geoff Coren sprung forwards and launched himself with his arms outstretched towards the pile of paper. But he wasn't quick enough. Cruncher's long neck swooped down and the llama grabbed the paper between his yellow teeth and began frantically munching. This was tasty paper.

Geoff Coren let out a wild banshee-like howl, leaped to his feet and began tugging at the paper that was still poking out of Cruncher's mouth. While the manager pulled one way, Cruncher pulled the other. The pair of them began dancing around the office in a strange expensive-contract tug-of-war. Neither was willing to budge.

Geoff Coren tried to judo sweep Cruncher's front legs but kept missing. The tiny manager's legs were just too short to make contact. This made Cruncher munch and swallow even more of the contract. Geoff Coren could see months and months of work slipping away down the llama's throat.

'You furry brute! You can't eat my contract: I'm Geoff Coren. The greatest manager ever. GIVE IT BACK!' he screamed.

Cruncher just kept chewing.

With all his might, Geoff Coren did one final heave on the corner of contract he had grasped in his hands. But Cruncher's firm, toothy grip was too strong – and there was an almighty RIIIPPPPPPPPPPPPPPPPPPPP.

Coren went flying backwards with a tiny useless corner of the contract in his hands. As he fell, he caught his heel on the edge of a huge Persian rug and tumbled into one of his heavy gold lamps. The top of the lamp wobbled and then came crashing down on his head. He was out cold.

Cruncher swallowed what was left of the contract with a satisfied gulp, did a quick wee on the plush white carpet and casually strode out of the room and into the corridor, taking a large bite out of huge painting of Geoff Coren that was hanging up by the door for dessert.

Tim and McCloud were just about to lead the remaining ten llamas back out on to the pitch for the second half when Tim heard a familiar voice call out to him. It was the thin man in the white suit with the colourful shirt.

'Hey, young fella!' the man shouted over the crowd of people near the tunnel. 'I've found your missing llama. He was just wandering down the corridor near our box.' He handed Tim the rope that he was leading Cruncher by. 'He seems to be OK,' continued the man, stroking Cruncher under the chin, which the llama clearly enjoyed. 'He was happily chewing his way through a load of paper. Hope it wasn't anything too important.'

Tim thanked the man perhaps too many times and gave Cruncher a big hug around the neck. Even though they were two–nil up, it was a huge relief to see him again.

'Nice llama you've got there. Great coat,' said the man, rubbing Cruncher's back. 'Anyway, good luck with the rest of the game. Hope you win. I can't stand Hotspurts.' He gave a cheery wave and disappeared back into the crowd.

Just then Cairo reappeared from his wandering round the ground. His hands were bright blue. I have no idea why.

'Oh great, you've found him,' he cried with a huge sigh of relief.

'Yes, a nice man I met in one of the boxes found him wandering about one of the corridors. But I have a feeling he had been locked in one of the offices by someone.'

'Probably by someone wanting to cheat us out of a place in the next round,' said Cairo with a frown. Then his face brightened. 'Doesn't seem to be working though does it? Two-nil already, wow!'

Tim nodded eagerly. It felt like his head was going to explode; he was so happy that his team had done so well even with all these obstacles being thrown in their path. 'C'mon, let's finish these cheats off,' he said, slapping Cairo on the shoulder.

Having Cruncher on for the second half made it even harder for Hotspurts, especially as their manager had gone missing. Goal Machine notched up another two goals and Llama United left the ground with a very comfortable 4 – 0 win under their belts.

It was only on the way home that it finally dawned on Tim what had happened that day. Cairo was already on his fifth bottle of celebratory cola.

'WE ARE IN THE SEMI-FINALS OF THE CUP!' Tim shouted.

'Wakey, wakey. That happened about two hours ago,' said Cairo.

'WE ARE IN THE SEMI-FINALS OF THE CUP!' Tim shouted again, grabbing Cairo and shaking him with delight. 'YIPPPPPPPPPPPPPPPP PPPPPPPPPPPPPPPPEEEEEEEEEEEEEEEEEEE EEEEEEEEEEEEEEEEEEEEEEEEEEE!'

'And we managed to get through even though Hotspurts cheated,' added Cairo. 'That won't happen again.'

Little did they know their semi-final opponents had an even nastier plan up their sleeves.

32
THE LUDO DISASTER

The semi-final of the Cup against Gunnerall was just a week away, and all of Tim's dreams were about football. In the good ones, Llama United always won the trophy, usually by loads of goals. But the bad dreams were really bad. The worst was when Tim had to play the game in goal, totally naked. Nobody would lend him a kit. He was so busy covering his crown jewels that he couldn't use his hands, so every time someone had a shot it would fly into the corner of the net. The crowd were laughing, the players were laughing, the coaching staff were laughing; even the royal person and their family sitting high up in the stand were laughing.

When Tim woke from that one he was drenched in sweat with his duvet wrapped round his neck. He let out a huge sigh of relief that it was only a dream and he wouldn't have to go in goal, especially not naked.

Tim put on his Llama United training kit. A black tracksuit, with purple trim, the Llama United badge and his initials – 'TG' – emblazoned across his chest. He was very proud of this kit; it made him look really professional. Beetroot had done a fantastic job making one for each person in the backroom staff, even though Frank had complained about the price. He then brushed his hair, which was rare because he didn't usually bother, and then went downstairs for some breakfast.

Oddly, Cairo was already in the kitchen. He had his head in his hands and he looked very sad. Tim had never seen him like this before.

'I've got some bad news, Tim,' said Cairo quietly.

'What is it?' asked Tim, a prickly feeling attaching itself to his neck.

Cairo let out a big sigh and sniffed away a tiny tear. 'Looks like Ludo got injured during the night. He's lying down in the middle of the field.'

Ludo *never* lay down. He was the ultimate standing-up llama. If there was a world record for standing up, Ludo would win it hands down . . . Well, feet down; llamas don't have hands.

'Oh no!' exclaimed Tim. 'What happened? Is he going to be all right?'

Cairo let out another huge long sigh, and did another big sniff.

'No idea what happened. McCloud found him like that this morning. Your dad has called the vet and she'll be coming in a bit.'

Tim sprinted out to the field. True enough, Ludo was lying on his side in the grass, breathing very slowly. The other llamas, plus Motorway, Frank, McCloud, Beetroot, Monica and Fiona were all standing around him in a big circle. Tim skidded down in the mud next to Ludo and gave his neck some strokes. Ludo just lay there, his dark dry tongue hanging out of his mouth slightly. His eyes were glazed over. The little look and nod he always gave Tim as a greeting wasn't there this time.

'How did this happen, Ludo?' whispered Tim, as a tear rolled down his cheek. 'Please don't die on us!'

Cairo knelt down next to Tim and started softly humming while stroking Ludo's neck. He didn't say anything but Tim could tell he was trying his hardest to hold back the tears.

So what did happen to Ludo? Well, if I'm honest, I wasn't paying attention and completely missed whatever happened in the field. I'm frightfully sorry about this. Luckily, I speak sheep, and I managed to listen in on Motorway muttering about the details. I'm going to summarize what she said below because her story is full of 'bleets' and 'baas', so it took ages.

Apparently, in the dead of night a red-and-white van pulled up and three men dressed in black hopped over the fence. One of them was carrying a huge metal bar and he swung it at Ludo several times. Luckily, Ludo somehow brilliantly kicked it away each time. This made the men angry, so one of them went back to the van and returned with a plastic bag. The other two men grabbed Ludo and stuffed whatever was in the bag down Ludo's throat. Ludo suddenly started coughing and spluttering and staggering about the field, then he lay down on the ground. The three men did high fives and then got back in the van and drove off.

Doesn't sound very nice does it? Well it wasn't. Cup football makes people do funny things.

As Tim stroked Ludo's neck, a woman in a smart red dress and sparkly black shoes clambered into the field. She was carrying a small leather case and she had a really wide grin on her face.

'Hiya,' said the smart woman, kneeling down in the mud. 'I'm Janet Guymond, the vet. This must be Ludo.'

Tim looked Janet up and down. She certainly wasn't dressed like a vet. She looked like she was going to work in an office. Janet noticed she was being eyed suspiciously.

'Oh, don't you worry about me, young man.' She laughed. 'I am a vet. I'm the "No Wellingtons Vet". You might have seen my adverts? I'm famous for not wearing wellingtons. Which was fine when I worked in the city, but it's not working quite as well now I'm in the countryside . . . I've ruined so many shoes . . .' She trailed off, noticing Tim and Cairo were only really interested in Ludo.

'So, let's see what's up with the patient. Don't

think I've ever done a llama before,' said Janet with a chirpy laugh.

This was not something Tim wanted to hear. He screwed up a little patch of grass in his fist in annoyance, but remained silent.

Janet did all the usual checks you would do on any animal; looked in his eyes, checked his mouth and ears, then his hair and limbs. Ludo remained unmoved. 'Hmmmm,' she muttered to herself as she began studying Ludo's dry tongue. 'This is unusually dry. What have you been feeding him?'

'Same as all the other llamas,' said Tim. 'Just the llama feed, hay and water, plus the grass of course.'

'Hmmmm, the grass,' said Janet, expertly pulling herself to her feet and patrolling the surrounding area like a detective. 'I think your llama might have been poisoned.'

'POISONED!' exclaimed Tim, Cairo, McCloud and Frank all at the same time, like people do in the movies.

'Yes, poisoned,' said Janet, stalking around the field. She was following a load of footprints in the mud. You've got the semi-finals of the Cup coming up in a few days' time. I'd say this was an act of sabotage . . . Aha!'

Janet bent down to pick something up off the ground. 'Here's the culprit.' She held some bright red packaging above her head.

'What's that?' asked Tim, his stomach clenched with fear.

'This is an empty packet of Jimmy Wodgers, the driest biscuit known to man. These biscuits can suck the moisture out of anything. They are especially deadly to pack animals that retain a lot of water, like the camel or llama.'

Tim grabbed the red packaging from the vet and ripped it into tiny pieces. This wouldn't make Ludo any better but he needed to take his fury out on something.

'It must be the work of Gunnerall,' said McCloud through gritted teeth. 'They'll try anything to get an advantage over us in the semi-final. Nobbling our goalkeeper is the lowest of the low.'

'But will Ludo be all right?' Tim asked Janet, ignoring McCloud's angry muttering.

The vet's face crunched into a frown. 'It's very hard to tell at this stage; it really depends on exactly when he was fed the biscuits. We'll do some tests. If it was longer than ten hours ago . . . he might not be able to play football ever again.'

Cairo buried his head in his hands; he was really crying now. Tim gave him a reassuring pat on the shoulder, but he was also having to blink a lot to fight back the tears. He looked down at Ludo and whispered softly in his ear.

'It's going to be OK, Ludo, we are going to get you through this. The vet is going to do some tests and make you better and you'll be back strutting round the field in no time. I promise.'

Frank pulled out his black notepad when he heard the word 'tests' – they sounded expensive. His badly built vineyard wasn't doing very well either. It turns out that grape vines don't really like the cold and the rain, so he had to keep replacing them, which was costing him even more money. Meanwhile, part of Fiona's princess castle had blown away one Wednesday morning, so she was in a really bad mood with him. Poor Frank.

'It's not all doom and gloom,' said Janet encouragingly. 'If we've caught the poisoning early he might make a full recovery, although he'll be a long-shot for the semi-final.'

Tim wiped his eyes on his sleeve. 'I'm not really bothered about whether he can play any more; I just want him to be all right. He was our first llama, after all.'

'That's the spirit,' replied the vet. 'I'll do my very best for him.'

'But what do we do if he doesn't make the semi-final?' said McCloud, his voice breaking. It sounded like he might burst into tears at any minute too.

Tim turned on his heels and stormed off. As he crossed the field he took several deep breaths to try and calm himself down; if he didn't he would lose his temper with the heartless McCloud. Right now, Llama United didn't matter. Ludo's health was more important than the semi-final.

33
THE SUBSTITUTE

On the Wednesday before the semi-final McCloud called a team meeting in the Gravys' kitchen.

Since the poisoning the family had taken it in turns to sit and keep an eye on Ludo at the vets. Even Fiona had spent a whole night reading her favourite books to him. Oddly these were mainly cookbooks. Cookbooks about puddings. I'm not sure llamas are impressed by jam roly-poly.

'I've been thinking about the game situation,' McCloud said as everyone settled into their seats. 'The game is only a few days away and Ludo hasn't recovered yet.'

'That's typical,' tutted Tim folding his arms. 'All you're thinking about is the match – you don't care about Ludo.'

Poor Tim was exhausted; he spent the most time alongside Ludo and had hardly slept. He'd get angry with himself if he ever nodded off and found himself jogging on the spot to keep himself awake. He was desperate to see a tiny flicker of recognition in Ludo's eyes.

McCloud shook his head. 'No, no, you are very wrong, laddie. I do care about Ludo. I care about him very much . . . that's why I've been thinking about forfeiting the match.'

'Really?' replied Tim. He'd always thought McCloud only cared about football, and the word 'forfeit' would never even enter his head. Maybe he wasn't so heartless after all.

McCloud nodded. 'Aye son, it's probably for the best that we cancel the match.'

It was Cairo who jumped in to stop the conversation. 'Hey, hey, you are talking like Ludo is dead. He's not, he's still alive. I doubt he'd want you to cancel the match just because he got injured. You've worked so hard to get to this stage, plus all the supporters are counting on you.'

'That's true,' replied Tim. 'We've also got to pay the bills on the farm.'

He looked at his dad, who had been silent so far. Tim knew he was thinking about the bills mounting up, and possibly grapes. He was nervously twisting that cursed little black notepad in his hands.

'So instead of being all miserable about it, let's think of a solution,' Cairo continued. 'You'd be really angry if Ludo got better again and you'd already cancelled the match. Couldn't we try and find a substitute keeper?'

'Where the Gable Endies are we going to get a substitute llama goalkeeper at this stage?' snorted McCloud. 'The game is just three days away. Even if we could find another guard llama, there's no guarantee they'd be any good at football.'

'It doesn't have to be a llama goalkeeper,' said Cairo. 'Just a goalkeeper. There must be someone. How about you, Frank?'

Frank shuffled uneasily in his seat. 'I'm rubbish at football,' he muttered. 'I can hardly even catch a beach ball.'

It's true. During his school days Frank was almost always picked last for football. It wasn't rare for the opposition to score more than ten goals when he was playing, which would usually mean he'd get loads of abuse, such as 'Hey, Gravy, you're the worst football player ever!' and 'My gran tackles better than you, Gravy!' – and that was just from the teacher. It still made Frank wince thinking about it now, thirty years

later. So the last thing he was going to do was go in goal in front of 80,000 people in the semi-final of the Cup.

'Ahem, ahem,' said Monica from the doorway. She was holding her laptop again.

'I think I might have found a solution,' she said with a grin.

Tim, McCloud, Cairo and Frank peered at screen. Several pictures of men wearing green or yellow tops were displayed in a long list.

GOALKEEPERS FREE AGENT LIST

RAY CLICK

Age: 34

League appearances: 127

Goals: 0

Honours: League Two title

Height: 6ft 2"

Weight: 13st 8

Click is famed for his point-blank one-handed save in the Cup third round against Bognor Regis, which saved Sathampton from a humiliating defeat to lower league opposition. Strong, reliable and injury free.

ALESSANDRO DI ALESSANDRO

Age: 26

League appearances: 10

Goals: 0

Honours: Italy U21

Height: 6ft

Weight: 12st 4

Despite a promising youth career Alessandro has

struggled with injuries over the last few seasons. However, he has now made a full recovery and is ready for a new challenge. Penalties a speciality.

JOE TOOT

Age: 40

League appearances: 6

Goals: 0

Honours: none

Height: 6ft 3"

Weight: 14st 6

Toot has been part of League Champions Munchester United's side since the early 2000s and has been a valuable and experienced second-choice keeper during a huge period of success. Handling and agility are important parts of his game.

DUNCAN O'LEARY

Age: 42

League appearances: 502

Goals: 6

Honours: Cup (3), Premier League (1), League Cup

(4), Ireland caps (87)

Height: 6ft 1"

Weight: 18st 10

As one of Ireland's favourite sons, Duncan O'Leary needs very little introduction. The man who single-handedly got Ireland into the quarter-finals of the World Cup after scoring the winner against Saudi Arabia in the first knockout stage. His well-publicized off-field problems have now been put well and truly behind him.

OLIVER WHIPSON

Age: 36

League appearances: 97

Goals: 0

Honours : none

Height: 6ft 4"

Weight: 14st 2

Following a five-year hiatus from the game, Whipson has returned to professional football after the collapse of his TV career. Command of area and leadership are his plus points.

'Wow, this is impressive,' said Frank, 'Well done, Monica. How did you get this?'

'Off the internet,' replied Monica with a shrug. 'You can get most things off the internet if you look in the right place.'

'Maybe we should start ringing their agents right now before someone else snaps them up,' said Cairo.

McCloud made a strangled coughing noise. 'Whooa, the Bully Wee, sonny,' he shouted. 'Hold your horses. There's a good reason why these players still don't have a club so late in the season.'

'Why's that?' asked Cairo.

'Because they are all rubbish and naebody wants them. This is the dregs of professional football right here, all made to look good by their agents so clubs will sign them.'

'But there's a bloke here with eighty-seven Ireland caps,' said Cairo, scrolling to Duncan O'Leary's face on the screen.

'C'mon, Cairo,' said Tim. 'Even my mum has heard of Duncan O'Leary. He's an absolute nightmare, has been since that World Cup. He's headbutted referees, kicked club owners and once he even punched a police horse!'

'Not forgetting that time he brought a whole bag

of goldfish on to the pitch and began eating them raw. He even spat the heads at the crowd. Not a pretty sight,' added McCloud, shaking his head in disgust.

'OK, OK,' said Cairo. 'Maybe not Duncan O'Leary, but how about Alessandro Di Alessandro? It says he is injury free now.'

McCloud chuckled knowingly. 'Aye, about as injury free as a badger that's just broken all four of its wee legs,' he said. 'He's famous for being injured all the time. He broke his hand pulling on his gloves, broke his foot kicking a ball, and even broke his own nose sneezing.'

Cairo scanned the list again. This was turning into the worst game of Guess Who ever. 'Er, Joe Toot?' he suggested.

'Old cry baby,' roared McCloud.

'Oliver Whipson?'

'TV star prima donna, always fiddling with his hair. Useless, the lot of 'em!'

'Well, that's everyone on this list apart from Ray Click,' said a resigned Cairo. 'You'll be telling me he has one eye and one foot or something I suppose.'

Tim and McCloud looked at each other.

'He was a fantastic keeper. One of the best,' said McCloud, slowly. 'But naebody has heard from him

243

in years. Something happened and he disappeared.' The old Scotsman rubbed his chin thoughtfully. In professional football, nobody would let a perfectly good keeper slip on to the scrapheap for no reason, so Ray Click's story worried him.

'Well, if Ludo doesn't get fit in time we need to have a plan B. Maybe Ray Click is our best and only option? Can you ring the agent right now?' asked Tim, handing McCloud the phone.

Frank let out a huge wail, as though he just learned that bacon sandwiches had been banned by the government. 'That's going to be more money, isn't it? Professional players are really expensive, aren't they?' He reached for his little black notepad and began scribbling in it. 'If this doesn't work, we'll all be eating hay next week!'

34
THE CURSE OF RAY CLICK

Now, who really wants to read about the contract wranglings of footballers? OK, let me just count: one, two, three, four and five. That's not enough to go into great detail, and this would have ended up being the most boring chapter ever. Let's skip ahead.

Frank was right, Ray Click would be expecting a big chunk of money to play: £5,000 a week, plus £7,500 for a clean sheet, £4,500 as a win bonus and £10,000 as a goal bonus – which was an odd request for a goalkeeper. Me, I would have been lucky to get a bag of humbugs and a stiff handshake when I played.

All this money would take a huge bite out of Frank's repayments to the bank. The Gravy family were already stretched to breaking point with the vet's daily fees before having to pay for a professional footballer. The small amount of money they'd earned from ticket sales and merchandise was pouring away

like fruit juice down Fiona's greedy throat.

If the spending carried on like this they would lose the farm straight after the Cup final, if they even got that far. Frank's little black notepad was now overflowing with maths, and not the good kind of maths. Instead it was full of subtraction and division sums. It was so full he had to buy another notepad, which cost him even more money.

When Frank wasn't watching, Tim sneakily wrote a positive motivational note on the inside cover:

The llamas are great. We are going to win the Cup and everything will be all right.
Oh, and I'd like a new games console for my birthday please.
Love Tim x

Before the semi-final at Old Trifford, Llama United received some mixed news from the vet. Ludo *would* make a full recovery from the biscuit poisoning, which was brilliant, but he *wouldn't* be fit for the semi-final. Tim's initial delight that Ludo was going to be back to his best was quickly replaced by butterflies in his stomach when he thought about whether Ray Click would be a good enough keeper to get them into the final. He could tell McCloud, Frank and Cairo were all worrying about the same thing. On the way to Old Trifford, hardly anyone spoke for the whole three-hour journey. Well, Cairo farted a few times, but I don't think that counts as talking.

Ray Click's agent had told them that the keeper would be waiting for them at the ground and wouldn't need any practice before the match.

As Tim and Cairo began warming up with the llamas, they noticed a man strutting up and down the middle of the pitch. He was tall and broad and was confidently walking around like he owned the place. Tim and Cairo eyed him suspiciously. He was dressed in expensive baggy jeans, thick black boots and a red basketball top, which showed off his muscular, tattoo-covered arms. He arrogantly swaggered across to Tim and Cairo and stood in front of them with his hands buried deep into his pockets.

'S'up,' the man said nonchalantly, as though he didn't have a care in the world.

Tim and Cairo didn't reply. They were transfixed by the man's tattoos. Apart from his face, every inch of him was coated in weird and wonderful ink. Dragons, skulls, serpents, flames, wildcats, birds and, unusually, fruit with legs prowled across his body and all the way up to under his chin.

'Cool, aren't they?' said the man. 'Cost me loads of money. But it doesn't matter 'coz I've got loads of money.' He waggled his hands in the air. His fingers had all manner of ugly, jewel-encrusted rings on them, while on his wrist he wore a chunky gold watch and various thick gold bracelets. 'These are very expensive also,' he said smugly, raising his jeans slightly to show the top of his gold plated boots.

Tim took an instant dislike to this show-off. Whoever he was, Tim knew that bragging about wealth wasn't a nice quality in a person.

'Is that . . . um . . . is that a *magpie*?' asked Cairo pointing at the nape of the man's neck.

'It sure is, boy,' the man said, grinning at Cairo with teeth so white that Cairo had to shield his eyes.

'That's my most recent tattoo. Right smart ain't it?'

Cairo frowned at the magpie. It was a truly hideous piece of artwork. Its fat black-and-white body was tattooed across the man's neck with its wings stretching across his shoulders. Clamped in its beak was a diamond necklace. Another horrible display of the man's obvious wealth.

'He's a cheeky one, that magpie. ''E's only gone and nicked someone's jewels,' said the man, laughing as though this was a good thing.

Cairo pursed his lips. Tim could tell he didn't like him either. 'Isn't one magpie supposed to be unlucky?' asked Cairo. 'You know, one for sorrow and all that.'

'Nah,' said the man confidently. 'That's a robin. Those nasty red-breasted things that pinch Christmas puddings when you're not looking.'

'Nope,' said Cairo, standing his ground. 'I'm sure it's a single magpie that's unlucky, right Tim?'

Tim hadn't a clue which birds were lucky and which were unlucky, but he backed up his mate all the same. 'Oh yes, very unlucky. Football is full of superstitions . . . magpies especially.'

The man shrugged and sucked his teeth. 'I'm supposed to be meeting someone called McCloud,' he said, changing the subject. 'Down here is he?' He pointed towards the tunnel and swaggered off.

Tim and Cairo stood open-mouthed as they watched the tattooed man walk away. The bad news was sinking in – this unpleasant fellow was Ray Click, their new and very expensive goalkeeper.

Something odd happened as Ray Click got to the edge of the pitch; he suddenly tripped over his own feet and crashed to the ground. With a look of surprise he got up, dusted himself down and then walked straight into the edge of the tunnel, banging his head. He shrugged to himself, touched the top of his head to check he wasn't bleeding and eventually disappeared off down the tunnel.

'Oh dear, oh dear, oh dear,' said Cairo. 'He's cursed!'

'Cursed?' replied Tim. 'What do you mean?'

'That magpie,' said Cairo anxiously. 'It's made him unlucky.'

'Don't be stupid, Cairo. That's just an old wives' tale.'

Cairo gave his best friend an incredibly serious look. 'Mark my words, Tim. This is a bad omen. A very bad omen. Ray Click should go nowhere near this football pitch.'

35
THE NEW KEEPER

There were just forty-five minutes left until kick-off. Tim could hear the roar of the crowd from above as he sat nervously under the stands, trying to eat the last few bites of the chocolate bar he had started an hour ago. He knew his dad had managed to sell at least a thousand tickets to Llama United fans, which wasn't that many but was still pretty impressive for just one very badly organized salesperson. Gunnerall fans had managed to snaffle the rest of the tickets, so the ground would once again be made up of a sea of people who wanted to see Llama United lose.

McCloud had told the media that Ludo had been injured during training and wouldn't be playing. This had made a lot of people very upset because Ludo had a cult following. Some of the Llama United fans had even created 'GET WELL SOON LUDO' flags to wave during the match.

McCloud was initially delighted to see Ray Click, but after a few seconds of conversation realized what an unpleasant man he was. Rather worryingly, when McCloud tried to shake Ray Click's hand the goalkeeper missed it. Then when Click went to sit on the bench he also missed that and fell on the floor. I'm just going to call him Click now because I don't like him either.

'Take him outside for a warm-up,' Cairo whispered to McCloud, as they watched Click struggling to get his feet into a pair of socks. 'I've got a funny feeling that something's not right.'

McCloud folded his arms and nodded. He too knew something was up. 'We're going for a warm-up, Click,' he bellowed. 'Follow me.'

'Yeah, whatever,' replied Click, picking up his gloves and then dropping them. He followed McCloud out of the changing room, banging into the door as he went.

McCloud and Click returned five minutes later. McCloud's face was grey; all the colour had drained from it. Click looked exactly the same as he had before . . . badly tattooed and arrogant.

'Would you step inside here, Click,' said McCloud,

opening the door to the large store cupboard in the corner of the room. 'Just need a quick chat.'

As soon as Click stepped inside the cupboard, McCloud slammed the door behind him and locked it from the outside. He turned to Tim and Cairo. 'Boys, that's the worst goalkeeper I've ever seen in my life. I've seen a one-day-old baby with more skill than Ray Click. He's totally lost any ability he ever had!'

'It's the curse of the magpie,' whispered Cairo to Tim.

Ray Click starting banging on the inside of the cupboard door and shouting about his wages for the match. Everyone ignored him.

'Right, we're in big trouble now, laddies,' said McCloud, pointing dramatically at the huge clock that hung above the changing-room door. 'Who's going to play in goal in a game that kicks off in under twenty minutes?'

Tim looked around the room. Click was locked in the cupboard; an incredibly expensive failure. Then there was Cairo; the worst football player he had ever met. And finally McCloud; an old man who struggled to bend down, let alone leap across a goalmouth and punch away a ball. Hang on, why were they both looking at him?

253

'Why are you staring at me?' he asked.

''Coz you're Tim Gravy and you're great,' replied Cairo with a cheeky smile.

Tim was confused. Then McCloud came over and put his arm round his shoulder, which McCloud never did . . . ever. Tim was even more confused.

'So, laddie,' began McCloud. 'Your friend Cairo is right. You are great.'

'Why are you both saying I'm great?' asked Tim suspiciously.

'Because you are,' shouted Cairo, throwing his arms into the air. 'Actually, you are one of the greatest, ever.'

'Greatest ever *what*? I'm not great at anything,' said Tim slowly . . . Then he twigged. McCloud was holding up a green number one jersey. 'Oh no, I can't . . . I can't go in goal in the semi-final of the Cup!'

Cairo and McCloud were both grinning at him and slowly crowding around him with the jersey. So, it seemed, were the llamas.

'I can't go in goal! I just can't. I'm just a kid!' said Tim, his voice breaking in terror. He could feel the room getting smaller and smaller, then . . . 'BBBBBBBBBBBBLLLLLLLLLLLLLLLLLL

EEEEEEEUUUUURGGGGGGHHHHHHHH!'

He puked all over the floor and fainted in a heap.

When Tim came round a few minutes later, he was wearing the green number one jersey, shorts, socks, boots and a brand-new pair of bright white goalkeeper's gloves.

He still felt sick and the room was spinning. Cairo was splashing flecks of water on to his face, while McCloud was lacing up his boots for him.

'Where am I?' asked Tim groggily.

'Ah, glad you're awake. You're in the same place you were ten minutes ago, old pal,' replied McCloud.

'You're about to be the first eleven-year-old to play in a Cup semi-final.'

'BBLLLLLUUUURRRRGGGGHHHHHHH!' Tim was sick again, but this time he didn't pass out.

'I've already changed the team sheet and handed it into the ref's office and it has been accepted,' said McCloud without a hint of emotion. 'I've also made you captain. This is the kind of pressure you should thrive on.'

'BBLLLLLUUUURRRRRGGGGGHHHHHHH!' went Tim again.

As a former professional footballer McCloud was used to pre-match nerves and all the stuff that goes with it. It wasn't anything new to him; it was normal, as was a player being sick before a match. He stepped over the mess on the floor, left the changing room and headed towards the dugout.

Tim dragged himself to his feet so he could look in the mirror. He was totally green; not just his jersey but also his skin. Cairo handed him a bottle of water to sip on.

'C'mon, Tim, you can do this,' his friend said encouragingly. 'I know it's a big game, but you've always been a great keeper when we've played together. Plus, you'll have the best back four in the country in front of you.'

'But I'm not that good,' wailed Tim. 'I'm just average, like I am at everything!'

'What are you talking about?' said Cairo in surprise. 'You are brilliant at loads of things. You've trained a team of llamas to play football, you've helped keep your dad's farm running, you've helped build websites, solved loads of problems, and you've been the best friend ever. You are definitely not average.'

Brian, Bill, Bob and Barcelona were standing proudly alongside their new keeper, looking determined and focused. Tim could feel some confidence filling his boots.

'Just pretend we are out in the field having a kick-about. It doesn't matter if Gunnerall score – Llama United will score more,' added Cairo.

Tim knew Cairo was trying his hardest to make him feel better, and it was working. Perhaps he wasn't that average after all. Playing in goal in a Cup semi-final was a massive job for a professional, let alone an eleven-year-old boy, but maybe he was just the kind of eleven-year-old who could pull it off?

He didn't have much more time to think about it as a loud bell rang in the corridor. It was time for the Cup semi-final to start.

36
GUNNERALL V
LLAMA UNITED

The Gunnerall coaching staff were grinning from ear to ear when they saw Tim take to the field with the ten llamas. They had clearly had a hand in Ludo's poisoning with the deadly moisture-sapping biscuits, and their plan had worked. They now got to play against an inexperienced eleven-year-old instead of a phenomenally talented llama keeper. It should be a cakewalk. (I don't think that cakes can actually walk. This is just another lazy football phrase.)

The crowd and the media inside the ground were totally baffled by the arrival of Tim in the Llama United goal. They were expecting the cursed Ray Click. The standard roar of the crowd had been replaced by thousands of whispers as fans discussed the new keeper. Beetroot screamed with shock at seeing her only son wander on to the huge, lush green pitch dressed like a goalkeeper. Monica burst into applause and shouted 'Go on Tim!' at the top of her voice. Fiona didn't look up; she was in the middle of a huge hot dog, and ketchup had dripped all the way down her top. Frank was still in the food queue . . . he'd forgotten Fiona's drink.

Tim's stomach was churning over and over, but luckily for him he didn't have anything else to sick up. He walked towards the goal and took his place between the sticks, running through a routine he had seen hundreds of other goalkeepers do before a match. Tap the side of the posts with the studs on the bottom of his boots, do some jumps, and then do some bobbing and weaving to warm himself up. He tried his hardest to block out the supporters that were just feet away from him in the stand behind the goal. They were all Gunnerall fan, and everything he could hear from them was totally unpleasant. But he would just have to put up with it for forty-five minutes before he could get to the relative safety of the other end of the pitch where the Llama United fans were sitting. There was a bigger patch of purple behind the goal than ever before. Beetroot and Molly had worked really hard on the merchandise, and it looked like a few hundred of the Llama United fans were wearing things that they'd made. This gave Frank some lovely

259

adding sums for his new little black notepad.

A low steady clap started to build from the middle of the Llama United fans. Monica was standing on her seat, leading the fans around her. The clap got steadily louder and louder and quicker and quicker until it became deafening. Quite a din from a group of fans who were totally outnumbered by Gunnerall supporters. Even though he was at the other end of the pitch, Tim suddenly felt a few inches taller.

'C'mon, you can do this,' he muttered, giving himself a couple of whacks in the chest with his fist.

The ref blew the whistle, and Gunnerall got the game underway. They liked to play a European style of football with a well-executed, tidy, short passing build-up from the defence, through the midfield and then on to the three goal-hungry strikers. However, it was Llama United's high-tempo pressing game that seemed to be reaping the rewards today.

In the first fifteen minutes, Cruncher, Smasher and the Duke had good chances to put Llama United into an early lead, but Gunnerall's defence and goalkeeper looked like they meant business and snuffed out the threats.

Tim felt pretty comfortable. He hadn't touched the ball, and all of the action was at the other end of the pitch. It was hard to tell exactly what was going on, but seeing the llamas perform so well made him feel much more confident.

But in the blink of an eye, Gunnerall suddenly took the lead. Their left-winger cut inside Llama United's Bill and zipped a beautiful slide-rule pass into the path of an onrushing striker, who slammed the ball past Tim and into the back of the net. Even if Ludo was fully fit, he wouldn't have stood a chance stopping that effort. 1 – 0 Gunnerall. Tim's first touch of the ball was picking it out the back of the net. All the confidence drained out of him; what a terrible start. The horrible sick feeling returned.

Llama United huffed and puffed throughout the rest of the half but couldn't break down the brilliant Gunnerall defence. This is what Gunnerall specialized in: taking a one-nil lead and then strangling the life out of the rest of the game. Gunnerall hardly left their half and, apart from the goal, Tim hadn't been troubled once. He paced up and down the edge of his area praying that his team would get back into the match.

In the changing room at half-time McCloud and Cairo were very encouraging and tried their hardest to gee up their team. They were playing well – it was just that luck wasn't on their side today. Goal Machine was being marked out of the match by one of the best defenders in the world and he looked exhausted.

'How am I getting on?' Tim asked Cairo.

'Absolutely fine, Tim,' replied Cairo. 'You couldn't have done anything about that goal, and really you've had nothing much to do.'

'Do I look like a professional goalkeeper?'

Cairo smiled. He could have easily said, 'No, you look like a tiny eleven-year-old child standing in a massive net, in a huge stadium full of fans.' But he didn't, because he was a good friend. 'You look every inch the professional goalkeeper, Tim,' Cairo said confidently. 'I'd totally forgotten you were only eleven.'

The start of the second half was very much like the first. Llama United attacked, attacked and attacked but couldn't find a way through the solid Gunnerall defence. Tim found himself leaning against the post watching the match. The Llama United fans behind him were the complete opposite of the Gunnerall fans at the other end. They were offering words of support and praising Tim for being so brave. Monica and Beetroot had managed to get down to the front and were telling him how well he was doing. He was starting to feel stronger and more confident with every minute that passed.

It was still one-nil to Gunnerall deep into the second half when the Duke latched on to a huge punt downfield by Barcelona and found himself clean through on the opposition goal. Before he had a chance to take a shot he was sent crashing to the ground by the Gunnerall's experienced Argentinian keeper.

'FOUL, REF!' screamed the thousand Llama United fans in the ground and the tens of thousands watching on TV.

The ref peeped his whistle as loud as he could and ran towards the goal pointing at the penalty spot. He quickly rummaged around in his top pocket and pulled out a red card, which he flourished at the Gunnerall keeper.

After taking off a striker, Gunnerall brought on their substitute keeper, who was the total opposite of the man he was replacing. He was a young Welshman who, like Tim, would be making his debut. He looked incredibly nervous as he pulled on his gloves and dashed on to the pitch to face the penalty. This was easily the biggest moment of his career so far. But Tim didn't care about how the other keeper felt; this wasn't the time to be nice.

'Blast it past him,' he shouted up the pitch, cupping his gloved hands to the sides of his mouth. 'He's got nothing!'

Goal Machine was ready to take the penalty. He hadn't had the greatest game, but he was about to put that right by smashing this home and levelling the game. The ball was placed on the spot, and Goal Machine marked out his run. The whistle blew and Goal Machine turned and pelted towards the ball. He always hit them high into the top left-hand corner and this one would be no different. Hang on . . . he changed his tiny llama mind just as he struck the ball, and went top right instead. OH NOOOOOOOOOOOOOOOO! The crowd couldn't believe it. The young Welsh keeper dived the right way and somehow got the tips of his fingers to the ball and flicked it over the crossbar and into the jubilant Gunnerall fans behind the goal. What a fantastic save!

The youngster was mobbed by his delighted teammates. Goal Machine stood on the penalty spot with his head bowed, shamefully nibbling on the grass. It looked as if he was scared to raise his head. The lethal goal-scoring llama was a just normal llama after all. Had he blown Llama United's big chance?

Tim fell to the ground in his six-yard area. Visions of that nasty bank manager taking the farm away from his family tumbled into his head. Was this the end of their Cup adventure?

Hang on . . . was that a whistle? Yes, there it was again, a shrill sound against the deafening roar of the crowd. It was the referee and he was pointing at the penalty spot again. The Gunnerall players surrounded him and began shouting in his face, but he calmly waved them away and continued to point at the spot. He wanted the penalty to be retaken; the keeper had moved off his line before the penalty had been struck.

When all the furious Gunnerall players had been cleared away, Goal Machine stood by the penalty spot again. He was casually chewing on a big lump of turf like he'd already forgotten he'd just missed a penalty. This is because the llama brain is nearly as small as the brains of some professional footballers. Tim put his hands over his eyes and turned his back on the match – he couldn't bear to watch another penalty, his nerves were shot to pieces. He listened to the crowd go quiet . . . then a peep on the ref's whistle . . . then . . . 'YEEEEESSSSSSSSSSSSSSSSSSSSSSS!'

The Llama United fans behind his goal erupted; Goal Machine had done it. Llama United were back on level terms. Tim leaped up and down around his penalty area like a frog on a trampoline. It felt like his head was going to explode.

As the huge clock at the top of the stand clicked round to 4.45 p.m. and the ref began checking his two watches, a mis-hit Gunnerall back pass gave Llama United an unexpected corner – the only proper attack they'd had since the retaken penalty. As the llamas lumbered into the Gunnerall area they were met by a thick wall of red-and-white shirts. Gunnerall had brought everyone back to defend the dead ball.

While Cruncher took an incredibly long time to set up taking the corner, Tim was crossing everything: fingers, hands, legs and feet. He looked up into air to say a little prayer to the footballing gods. Then he noticed Cairo frantically waving his arms from the Llama United technical area – he was pointing at the Gunnerall goal.

'Go up for the corner,' said a clear voice from the crowd behind him, it was Monica.

'Yeah, go up for the corner,' shouted Beetroot. 'There's nothing to lose . . . the ref will blow for full-time if it's cleared!'

'What they say!' shouted Fiona. Frank had bought her a meat pie and she was greedily trying not to burn herself on the molten filling.

The crowd began to rumble out a loud chant: 'TIM . . . TIM . . . TIM . . . TIM . . . TIM . . . TIM!'

As I've said before, the Llama United crowd weren't the best at thinking up songs. This wasn't very good either, but it had the desired effect. Without really thinking about it, Tim found his legs had broken into a sprint up the field. He was running as fast as he'd ever run before up the vast green pitch.

Cruncher was now ready to take the corner. He hadn't noticed Tim charging up the pitch so didn't wait for him to arrive. His corner hung in the air for ages and then landed in the middle of thick huddle of llamas and Gunnerall players. The keeper had come out in a vain attempt to catch the cross, had missed it, and was already on the floor among the mud and boots. The ball pinballed around the area for a good few seconds before anyone could lay a solid foot on it. Sadly for Llama United, that person was a Gunnerall defender, who whacked it as far as he could away from their goal. The Llama United fans let out a huge disappointed sigh.

It wasn't the greatest clearance, but it was enough to get it out and away from the area . . . to exactly where Tim had finally arrived. He had run so fast it felt as though his heart was going to explode out of his chest. He was puffing and gasping for breath so much he hardly noticed the ball float towards him and hit him square on his belly. The impact took all the pace off the ball, and it fell towards the ground. Instinctively, Tim closed his eyes and swung his right foot at the ball in the vain hope he'd volley it back towards the goal.

He hit it sweetly. He could just tell – the ball felt perfect as it left his boot, and the sound was like a thousand angels singing. Everything seemed to go in slow motion as he opened his eyes and watched the ball sail over everyone's heads and finally . . . amazingly . . . nestle in the top corner of the net. 2 – 1. What a goal!

Tim's ears nearly fell off with all the screaming and shouting in the ground. McCloud, Cairo and most of the llamas leaped on top of him in the biggest celebratory bundle ever. Even Monica and Beetroot sprinted on to the pitch to join in. Blimey, they were heavy. Frank was so excited, he knocked Fiona's pie out of her hands while dancing on the spot and had to go off to buy her another one.

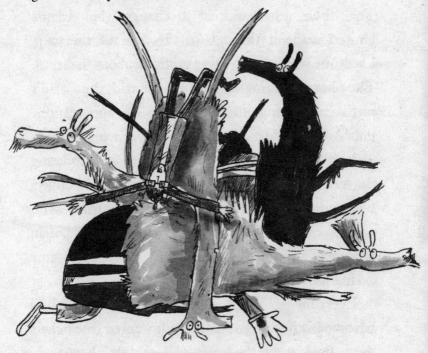

The final whistle blew. Llama United had done it. They were in the final of the Cup.

37
FRANK'S WIN BONUS

The whole world seemed to change when Llama United made it through to the final of the Cup. Everyone wanted to know everything about the team. The phone was ringing off the hook with the world's media requesting interviews and TV appearances. Poor Monica had hardly slept in the last week, she was so busy dealing with all the enquiries and updating the website and social media accounts. They'd done a few media things in the earlier rounds but this was on a different level. Tim was interviewed by a Brazilian journalist at 3.00 a.m., who spent most of the time asking him about cheese.

Everyone at Tim's school suddenly wanted to become his best friend as they all wanted free tickets to the final, as did the teachers. Tim didn't have to do a stitch of homework all week and his arm started to get sore with the amount of waving and handshaking he was having to do all day. Walking from the school gates to the classroom could take anything from ten to twenty minutes, when it usually took twenty-five seconds. Everyone wanted a piece of him.

McCloud wasn't happy with all the 'off-field distractions', as he called them. He refused to do any interviews and spent a lot of time hiding his face under a blanket like a criminal when he was doorstepped by TV camera crews. He was only happy when he was stood in the field with the llamas, training them. By the Monday of Cup final week, he had set up camp in the field and was living in a tent. He had also armed himself with a baseball bat and motorcycle crash helmet. If anyone trespassed on the field he would come flying out of the tent, usually totally naked, waving the baseball bat about like a lunatic. Journalists and nosy parkers soon got the message.

The llamas, on the other hand, were totally not bothered by the increase in adulation. Fans had been sending them presents for weeks, but most of them were useless to a llama. What can a llama do with a new juicer and some hand soap? They watched the media circus outside the field with the same 'so what' look on their faces that they'd had on since the start of the Cup journey.

Even though he hadn't been at the semi-final, Ludo seemed to be even closer to Tim than ever. He was well on his way to making a full recovery, but there was something different about him. He spent a lot more time walking alongside Tim in the field, like he was Tim's personal bodyguard. This obviously didn't please Motorway – she would bleet and baa at the top of her voice when Tim and Ludo went on long walks together.

Cairo remained cool throughout the Cup final build-up. He tried to take Tim's mind off the match by chatting about things that had nothing to do with football whatsoever. For example, who really likes sprouts? And why haven't they made a TV programme about hamsters? To be honest, Cairo was as nervous as everyone else; he was just trying to be strong for Tim.

Frank was *still* fretting about the farm. He had wasted money on beekeeping, the vineyard and Fiona's princess castle, which were all big failures. However, he had managed to keep the bank at bay thanks to the regular payments from the small number of ticket sales he had made and Beetroot and Molly's excellent merchandising. He could probably have made a lot more money if he'd known how to run a football club properly, but the Governing Body, TV companies and rival clubs had sneakily tricked him out of making any extra cash because it was obvious he didn't have any idea what he was doing. He didn't know that he should have got money for the matches being on telly, or that tickets aren't usually sold on a first-come, first-served basis. All this meant that after the Cup final had finished, the money stream that was keeping the farm afloat would finally run out.

Frank was seriously worried that he could end up in the unusual situation of winning the Cup but still having the bank take his farm away. On the Tuesday before the Cup final he was busy doing more sums in his new little black notepad when the phone rang.

'Can I speak to the owner of Llama United?' came the chirpy female voice at the other end of the phone.

'I suppose that's me,' replied Frank. 'I'm Frank Gravy.'

'Hello, Mr Gravy. I'm Cheryl Bogninnio . . .' She paused as though she was waiting for Frank to instantly recognize who she was.

'Er, hello, Cheryl.' Frank didn't have a clue who she was.

'I'm the chief executive of the global sportswear

firm Pike, and I have a proposal for you I'd like you to think over.'

Cheryl was renowned for being one of the toughest negotiators in the world and had been known to cancel huge deals because the coffee in the meeting was a little bit cold or because they had served custard creams. She hated custard creams . . . and bourbons . . . and ginger nuts. Actually, she hated every biscuit.

Cheryl also worked very quickly. In a world where companies can take months just to decide what fizzy drinks they should put in their vending machines, Cheryl liked to do all her deals within an hour.

'Get it done' was her and Pike's motto – and she lived by it.

'OK, I'm listening,' said Frank.

'If Llama United win the Cup on Saturday afternoon, Pike will give you half a million pounds.'

Frank did a tiny gasp and flumped down in the nearest chair in shock.

'Mr Gravy, did you hear me?' continued Cheryl. 'Half a million pounds, and all you need to do is win the Cup.'

Frank pulled himself together. Nobody could really get half a million pounds for just winning the

Cup; there had to be a catch. 'Well that sounds very interesting Miss . . . er, Cheryl,' garbled Frank. 'But there must be a catch.'

Cheryl laughed falsely again. 'No, no, there's no catch, Mr Gravy . . . of course I would gain exclusive rights to Llama United and be able to use them to promote Pike equipment for the foreseeable future. We could have Llama United shirts, boots, duvet covers, computer games . . . the list is endless.'

'They don't wear boots,' said Frank.

'Who cares, Mr Gravy! The public wear boots and will be happy enough to buy Pike-branded Llama United boots by the boatload.'

Frank paused for a bit of a think. All these months of financial worry would be over. Half a million pounds would easily save the farm, and he didn't have any problems with the llamas being used to sell stuff. He'd actually quite like some Llama United tea towels.

'You have thirty seconds to make your decision, Mr Gravy, or the offer is off the table!' barked Cheryl.

Frank didn't need thirty seconds. 'We'll take it,' he said firmly.

'Fantastic news, Mr Gravy,' said Cheryl, becoming warm again. 'I will have someone draw up a contract and whisk it round to you before the match. Just one thing though . . . if they lose, the deal is off.'

'Oh . . . OK then,' said Frank hesitantly. He knew Tim believed the llamas could win, so he'd have to believe it as well. After all, they couldn't afford to lose.

38
PRE-MATCH NERVES

The weather for Cup-final day was perfect. Tim sat quietly in the front of the transportation van watching the world go by as they drove to the stadium. It was the only thing that seemed to calm his horrendous nerves. It felt as though someone had snuck into his room in the middle of the night and poured twenty-five tanks of butterflies into his stomach. He couldn't eat breakfast or get his brain to focus on anything else other than the football match that was just a few hours away.

Ludo had completed his recovery and would play in goal. His regular long walks around the field with Tim had helped to build the llama's strength. In addition, Beetroot had constructed a very light training routine that got him back to the peak of fitness just in time.

Tim was thrilled that he wouldn't have to go in

goal again. Even though he had enjoyed being on the pitch, he knew he was lucky. He'd hardly had to make a save and his goal was a total fluke, so it was unlikely to happen again. Besides, Ludo was a better keeper, more experienced, and he wouldn't be sick before the game.

As the van snaked its way into the city and towards the ground, the occasional person would notice it and do a friendly wave or thumbs up. Tim would try and wave back politely but any sudden movement made him feel sick. Ugh, this was an awful feeling.

Cairo, McCloud and Frank all seemed equally nervous. Apart from more farts from Cairo, they'd hardly spoken for the whole journey. The farts were especially stinky today.

It was actually the first time that Tim thought having Fiona in the van would have lightened the mood a little. No, hang on; she would have been really annoying and would have added more farts.

When they arrived at the stadium it was already bustling with people waving huge flags for both teams. Tim had never seen anything like it. Some of the flags had the faces of the llamas on them. Loads of people seemed to be wearing his mum's Goal

Machine T-shirts and stripy scarves. Some fans were even wearing huge llama masks.

Wombley Stadium was definitely on a different level to all the other grounds Tim had been to on this Cup journey. Thousands and thousands of seats as far as the eye could see, a huge roof, and an arch so high that Tim could hardly fathom how big it was. He felt like a tiny speck of dust in a massive cauldron. Even though the fans hadn't been let in the ground yet, the atmosphere was already electric. It sent a big shiver down his spine . . . then he felt sick again.

McCloud appeared at his shoulder, taking in loud gulps of air. 'Suck that in, laddie,' he bellowed. 'This is hallowed ground. The best football pitch in the whole world.'

'Have you played here?' asked Tim.

'Aye, lad,' replied McCloud quickly. 'Way back in the seventies we beat England here in their own back yard. Two-one was the score and I got the winner. The crowds went mad that day and tore down the posts.'

Tim had known McCloud long enough now not to question his stories, even though he was never sure if they were true or not. Anyway, back when McCloud was a player, dinosaurs had still roamed the planet.

Hey, whoa there, I've just realized that I've totally forgotten to mention who Llama United were playing in the final. It was Munchester United: one of the biggest teams in the world and the team that Tim had wanted to play since the start of the Cup. They'd won hundreds of trophies in the past, so coming to Wombley was a pretty normal event for them. Luckily for Llama United, they weren't a team who needed to resort to underhand tactics like Gunnerall and Enfield Hotspurts because they were *so* good at what they did they rarely lost. They had five England internationals, three Spaniards, an Italian defender, a Brazilian midfielder and a German keeper. Fans would argue that they were all the best players in the world in their positions, and it was hard to go against that. In computer games they all had ninety ratings.

As a player I nearly joined Munchester United once, but my pet hedgehog at the time didn't like to travel, so we had to stay put. I think my footballing career could have been even better if it hadn't been for that hedgehog.

Munchester United were managed by a softly spoken Belgian who had already won the World Cup three times. Yes, that's right, with Belgium. What's that? Belgium have never won the World Cup? Sorry, but I haven't got time to discuss this; I've got a match to tell you about.

Munchester United's manager was an expert in tactics and always had huge files of info on every team that they faced. Llama United would be no exception. This was a big step up from the semi-final, and Llama United would need to be in tip-top form today.

'Do you think we can win?' said Tim to Cairo as a small trickle of colourful fans began filing into the stands and noisily taking their seats.

'I don't see why not,' replied Cairo. 'We've got this far; nothing is impossible.'

'It's just that I'm worried everyone knows everything about Llama United now,' said Tim. 'I've heard their manager has tactics worked out in perfect detail to face any side. We don't even have any tactics.'

'Don't we?' said Cairo in surprise. 'I thought McCloud did all that?'

'Well, I've never seen them. I think he just keeps them in his head.'

'Look, don't worry about that,' said Cairo.

'Remember, only me and you know the real truth about these llamas. They are fuelled by the ashes of Arthur Muckluck – the best footballer in the world. I don't think tactics really matter.'

The stadium was getting really full now. Most of the seats were filled with the red and white of Munchester United supporters, apart from a patch of purple-striped Llama United fans behind one of the goals. There were two thousand llama fans in attendance this time; Frank had worked extra hard selling tickets over the last couple of weeks. Right in the thick of it all were the six original fans – Pete, Tiny Pete, Steve, Kev, Warren and Tracey – who were thoroughly enjoying their day but were always quick to point out that they had been there for Llama United's first ever away match back in November.

The posh seats in the ground were filled with some of the most famous and richest people in the country. In just one box alone were Five Jackets, an award-winning actor, a multibillionaire businessman, a WWE wrestler, a military general and three TV chefs.

All the managers from the teams Llama United had beaten in the earlier rounds were also here, including

Geoff Coren, who was deep in conversation with some very angry-looking farmers. What a mixed bag of people. Beetroot, Molly, Fiona and Frank also sat up in the posh seats. But not Monica – she was in the middle of the sea of Llama United fans, dressed from head to toe in purple and with her face painted. She was once again leading the crowd in their slightly uninteresting array of songs. I must say, I quite liked the slow hand-clap from the semi-final; I hope they do that again.

A marching band stomped on to the pitch and began their musical routine. If the atmosphere was electric when the stadium was virtually empty, it was positively super-charged now.

Llama United looked spectacular in their freshly washed kit. Beetroot, Molly, Monica and Cairo had worked really hard on getting the team spotless for the match. They had trimmed their toenails, brushed their teeth and washed their hairy bits. The full back, Bob, had somehow persuaded Cairo to give him a Mohawk haircut and spent the entire warm-up admiring himself in one of the changing-room mirrors.

Tim could feel his breakfast beginning to rise in his stomach, but he hadn't had any breakfast – it

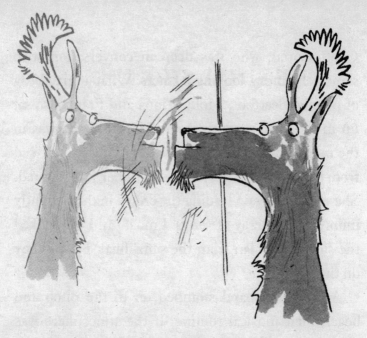

must have been all the breakfasts he had over the last
month trying to escape through his mouth instead.
And this was before a ball had been kicked.

What was he going to be like when the whistle blew?

39
THE FINAL SHOWDOWN

The noise from the crowd reached fever pitch as the ref blew the whistle to start the match. Munchester United kicked off and were zipping the ball about the lush green turf – the llamas couldn't get anywhere near it.

Wow, Munchester were good. They looked dangerous every time they attacked. Their little Brazilian midfielder, Poopo, was dictating the tempo of play and was just too tricky for the llamas. Poor old Brian brought him crashing down to earth with a nasty foul on the edge of the area, but the Brazilian hopped back up like a spring and quickly snapped the resulting free kick into the top left-hand corner of the Llama United goal. Ludo got nowhere near, it was so good. The red-and-white chunk of the crowd went wild.

It was Munchester United 1 – 0 Llama United.

Tim put his head in his hands and let out a huge sigh. There was plenty of time to get back in the match but this wasn't the best start. He leaped out of his seat, stormed into the technical area and swirled his arms around like a windmill. To Tim this meant 'Come on lads, let's pick this up'. To the llamas this meant 'Oh look, there's that boy waving his arms about again'.

Llama United didn't let their heads drop and they hit back almost instantly. Dasher made a brilliant break down the right, beating three Munchester players for sheer pace and guile. She then whipped in a perfect cross for the Duke, who climbed above the Munchester defence to head home the equalizer: Munchester United 1 – 1 Llama United.

Ten minutes gone and we'd already had two goals! What a match this was going to be.

Not for the first time, I was horribly wrong with my match prediction. The rest of the first half was just a flurry of crunching midfield tackles and misplaced passes. The less we talk about it the better.

Munchester United came flying out of the traps after the whistle was blown for the second half. They nearly scored straight from kick-off but Ludo pulled off a stunning diving-header save from Poopo's twenty-yard blaster.

Then disaster struck. Munchester made it 2 – 1. After a mega scramble in the Llama United area, the ball bounced kindly for Munchester's England captain, Dwain Mooney, to stab the ball home from five yards. Tim's head slumped forward so far that his chin hit his chest. But McCloud was much more animated.

'Plenty of time left, lads,' he shouted across the pitch, clapping his hands together. 'Pick it up, pick it up.' He looked at the depressed Tim. 'You too, sonny. Don't be down in the dumps; we've got this.'

He was right. Llama United started coming back at Munchester straight away. Dasher hit the post, the Duke was twice denied by the German keeper from close range, and Cruncher was inches away from getting the equalizer with a near-perfect twenty-five-yard lob.

But it wasn't enough . . . and unfortunately luck was on Munchester's side today. Lightning totally misjudged a header, which allowed one of Munchester's Spanish stars to nick in and dink the ball past Ludo, and before you could say, 'Hey! How did that happen?' it was Munchester United 3 – 1 Llama United.

Now Llama United had a huge mountain to climb. I hear that llamas are quite good on mountains though.

Even though it all looked lost, Llama United had an unlikely hero in their ranks: the full back, Barcelona. He'd had a fairly average game so far; he hadn't made many mistakes and had dished out a few solid tackles. In the eighty-second minute he suddenly went on a little run down the left side, his tongue flapping from side to side – it went on and on and on. The run, not the tongue. Even he couldn't believe just how far up the pitch he was when he saw the Munchester goal just yards away and the Duke lumbering around in the area.

Barcelona pulled back his front left leg and delivered one of the best crosses of his life, right on to the top of the Duke's head. The big llama rose majestically over the two Munchester centre backs and planted another thumping header into the corner of the net.

Munchester United 3 – 2 Llama United.

They were back in it, but had only eight minutes to get the equalizer. Tim and Cairo hugged briefly and then sprang towards the side of the pitch to shout more words of encouragement to the llamas. They needed another goal desperately.

The clock on the main scoreboard had stopped at ninety minutes, and the fourth official had raised his stoppage-time board. Three minutes, it read, in large orange digital numbers. This was last chance saloon for Llama United.

Ludo hoofed a huge clearance downfield. The entire Llama United team chased after the ball, including Ludo. The Munchester United midfielder who was first to it was barged out the way by Smasher, who won the ball with a terrific tackle. He then played a neat pass to Lightning, who zipped down the right and dribbled round two Munchester players. She then played a neat one-two with Bob, who had appeared from right back, and then arrowed in a cheeky little cross to the Duke, who flicked the ball back across the area. It was poetry in motion.

The ball bounced just once and there – stealing in at the far post – was Goal Machine, just the kind of llama you want in this situation, who dived full length across the six-yard box and headed the ball past the leaping keeper and into the net!

The crowd went totally wild. Tim and Cairo went totally wild. McCloud even broke into a little dance. The exhausted Munchester United players sunk to their knees. Llama United had done it; they got the equalizer in the last minute. The game was going to extra time . . . hang on . . .

In the far corner of the pitch stood a man dressed in black. He had his arm up in the air. In his hand was a flag, which was fluttering in the light wind. It was the linesman and the dreaded offside flag. It wasn't the flag's fault, to be honest. He didn't know he was being used to ruin one of the most spectacular Cup finals of all time. He'd originally hoped for a quiet life being a corner flag at a primary school. But no, his older brother on the other side of the pitch had pushed him to dream big, hadn't he? Well, now look what he had done.

It took nearly everyone in the ground some time to realize that the linesman had raised the offside flag. When they did, the cheers turned to boos very quickly. Even the referee seemed upset as he blew his whistle and indicated a free kick for Munchester United.

McCloud lost his temper and charged down the side of the pitch to confront the linesman. The Llama United coach was bright red and was waving his arms around uncontrollably.

'What the Doonhamers was that?! That's a

disgrace!' he barked, inches away from the linesman's face. The linesman took a step backwards, mainly because he was getting sprayed with the angry Scotsman's spit. However, he was experienced in dealing with angry managers so this was fairly common for him.

'Free kick . . . offside,' he replied calmly and jogged away.

'OFFSIDE?! OFFSIDE?!' shouted McCloud. 'WHAT THE ACCIES FOR? HE WASN'T OFFSIDE! If that's offside then I'm a panda bear.' It was the first animal that popped into his head.

The linesman continued to look away from the raging McCloud. 'His neck and head were offside. Now return to the dugout before you are sent to the stands . . . and take your bamboo with you.'

'HIS NECK?! HIS NECK!' screamed McCloud.

Tim ran towards McCloud to try to calm him down, but he was brushed away as the wild manager continued to chase the linesman up and back down the line.

'C'mon McCloud, you've got to stop,' he shouted in his ear. 'Come away, come away.'

The ref had now joined in, blowing his whistle frantically, obviously after being signalled by the linesman. 'You! Off.' He produced a red card from his top pocket and brandished it at McCloud, pointing up at the stands.

McCloud shouted 'HIS NECK!' one more time at the top of his voice, and with the help of Tim, Cairo, a few stewards and a couple of Munchester United players, he was escorted away from the linesman and off into the stands.

Seconds after that, the ref had had enough and he blew the final whistle. It was all over. Llama United were finally beaten.

Munchester United 3 – 2 Llama United.

Tim sank to his knees, his head bowed low against his chest. His stomach felt like he had just swallowed a safe. Not one of those tiny key-lock safes, but a big one like they keep in banks.

The red-and-white Munchester fans were delighted and hugged and celebrated like fans do when their team wins things.

The Llama United fans did a final chant of 'LLAMA UNITED, LLAMA UNITED!' and dejectedly filed out of the stadium, leaving Monica slumped in her seat, her face paint smudged with tears.

Tim and Cairo went round their team and offered them strokes and pats of support as the exhausted llamas hung their necks low to the ground. Both boys were bravely trying to hide the tears in their eyes. The adventure was over.

McCloud, Tim and Cairo solemnly led the team up the stairs to collect their runners-up medals, and then were forced to stay on the pitch as the Munchester United players lifted the trophy and danced about in front of their delighted fans.

It was really hard to watch. Well, it was for Tim, Cairo and McCloud. Motorway and all the llamas,

apart from one, were now one hundred per cent focused on eating the lush green grass of the Wombley pitch. Ludo had made his way across to Tim and was making a comforting humming noise next to him. The big llama knew his young friend was incredibly upset.

In the stands, where all the celebrities had been sitting, sat a man with his head in his hands. It was Frank. He had just lost half a million pounds, and with it his farm.

40
MR POLSTER

A few days later, Frank sat down with his entire family, plus Cairo, Molly and McCloud, to explain the grim situation. The money they had received from the Cup final would run out in a few weeks and he would have to sell the farm and the llamas. Everyone was heartbroken by the news. The last year had been tough but brilliant, and had now come to a horrible, crushing end.

The Gravy children were even more upset when they discovered that they were going to have to move in with Frank's sister in Scotland until he could find a new job. Fiona had recently learned a swear word at school and she said it a lot of times. Beetroot told her to stop using it immediately, but she still muttered it under her breath for a few more minutes.

'I can't believe we have to sell the llamas as well,' cried Tim. 'Can't we take them with us to Scotland?'

'Where would they go?' replied Frank. 'There's nowhere to put them at my sister's.'

'I'd take them at the animal shelter, but I just don't have the space,' said Molly sadly. 'It wouldn't be fair on the llamas or the other rescue animals. Especially the goats.'

'Besides, it wouldn't be the same if you weren't here to train them and help me with my rubbish football skills,' added Cairo, his bottom lip wobbling.

'But what about the llamas' football skills? Surely a football team would want to buy them?' cried Tim.

'There was a rumour that Royal Modrid wanted to buy Goal Machine,' said McCloud. 'But I had a talk with Molly, and we don't think he'd like to be separated from the rest of the team.'

'There must be something we can do?' said Tim. 'We can't just give up like this!'

'Sorry Tim, but I've gone through everything with your mother a hundred times,' said Frank sadly. 'The bank will take the farm and we'll probably have to sell everything that comes with it, which includes the llamas.'

The room went silent as everyone let the bad news sink in. Then there was a sharp knock-knock at the door. Frank went to answer it. This is a lucky coincidence isn't it? Although it would be a bit boring if someone had knocked on a Wednesday afternoon when everyone was out.

'Hullo there,' said the man at the door. He was dressed in a smart lime-green suit that, despite its colour, looked really expensive. 'Is Tim in?'

Frank showed him into the kitchen, where Tim had put his head face down on the table to stop himself from crying in front of everyone.

'This man is here to see you, Tim,' said Frank. Tim looked up and peered at the man through his watery eyes.

'Remember me?' asked the man with a grin. Tim didn't react. He was sure he didn't usually meet men who wore expensive lime-green suits.

'I'm Thomas Polster,' said the man. 'We met briefly at the Enfield Hotspurts ground. I found the missing llama in the corridor . . . remember?'

Tim sniffed, but before he had a chance to speak Beetroot had leaped up and was homing in on Mr Polster.

'Wow! Thomas Polster. *THE* Thomas Polster in my kitchen,' she squawked excitedly. The man nodded modestly. 'Can you believe Thomas Polster is in my kitchen?'

Tim and Cairo looked at each other and pulled 'What is she talking about?' faces. They had no idea who Thomas Polster was.

'Whooa! Whooa!' shouted Monica. 'Thomas Polster is in our kitchen!'

'I seem to be, yes,' replied Thomas Polster, looking slightly overawed by all the fuss that was being made of him.

'Wow, Thomas Polster,' Monica said again as she began touching the corner of his suit jacket, like someone who had just discovered the invention of material.

Thomas didn't seem to mind this intrusion into his personal space.

Tim and Cairo just stood there smiling, pretending to know who Thomas Polster was, but both were too polite to ask the 'Who are you?' question. He was clearly a big deal.

'Who the purple parrots are you?' chirped Fiona from beside the fridge. She had been trying to drink as much apple juice as possible before anyone had noticed, so hadn't been able to talk until now. She began hopping up and down straight away. She really had drunk a lot of juice.

'I sometimes make clothes,' replied Thomas.

'It's a bit more than that,' added the fawning Beetroot. 'He's the biggest fashion designer in the whole of Britain!'

'Probably in the whole of the world, Mum,' interrupted Monica.

Thomas Polster blushed as he tried to shrug off the praise.

'I don't like his jacket,' said Fiona loudly. 'It's a

horrible colour.' Then she left for a much needed wee.

'So why do you need to see me?' asked Tim. 'I don't know anything about fashion.'

'Well, to be honest, Tim, it's not really you I want.'

'Oh, OK,' said Tim, his shoulders slumping back down.

'It's actually your llamas I'm interested in,' Thomas continued.

'They're not for sale,' replied Tim quickly. 'We might try again for next year's Cup.'

Frank coughed. 'They might be for sale at the right price.'

'Dad!' cried Tim. 'We can't sell them. I won't let you!'

'We don't have any money, Tim. I thought I'd explained this. We are going to have to sell things.'

Thomas Polster smiled warmly. 'Don't worry, don't worry. I'm not here to buy your llamas. It's their wool I'm after.'

'The wool?' replied Tim. 'But it's all worn out from all the football they've been playing.'

'Quite the opposite, actually. When I stroked that llama in the corridor at Enfield Hotspurs I couldn't believe how soft it was. I can't find a soft fibre like that anywhere, and I've looked. I could make all sorts of garments out of it. Plus, you've got the added marketing value of the wool coming from Cup finalists. We'll sell out in no time.'

'Really?' said a disbelieving Frank.

'Really,' said Thomas Polster. 'In fact I believe it so much I'm willing to make you my regular wool supplier. How does one hundred thousand pounds a year sound? That should help you keep your farm, shouldn't it?'

Frank, Cairo, McCloud, Beetroot, Molly and Monica were speechless.

'But can they still play football?' asked Tim urgently, his tummy was excitedly flipping over and over.

'Of course!' said Thomas with a grin. 'I think that's what has been helping make their coats so soft.'

'Can we set up a football academy and make Llama United a proper team who might compete in a league or even in Europe?' added Cairo, who had absolutely no interest in fashion whatsoever. 'Can you make that happen as well? It would be sad to waste their talent on just clothes.'

The fashion designer shrugged and then a big grin spread across his face. 'I don't see why we can't do that. It would be good for the llama clothing brand.

301

Why don't I sponsor the team as well?'

Tim and Cairo were wide-eyed with excitement at the prospect. Frank gently put one arm around Beetroot's shoulder and let out a huge sigh of relief. With his other hand he took his little black notepad out of his pocket and threw it out of the window. McCloud sat down at the table, his bottom lip quivering with uncharacteristic tears of joy. Monica, meanwhile, was still clearly trying to come to terms with meeting Thomas Polster; she'd gone all pink and sort of floppy.

'So then, what do you say everyone?' pleaded the fashion chief, looking at the dumbstruck bunch of people in front of him.

'I say: it's a deal,' announced Fiona from the doorway of the room. She marched across the kitchen and shook Thomas Polster firmly by the hand. 'It's been a pleasure doing business with you. Now, make me a beautiful llama-wool coat . . . right now.'

EPILOGUE

A month later Tim and Cairo stood by a large bonfire melting marshmallows on the end of sticks. It was a Friday night, if you are interested.

The fire crackled and popped as it struggled to burn the pile of junk that had been hurled on to it. Flames licked the sides of some beehives, the vineyard fencing and a terrible-looking princess castle. Perched on the top were Frank's two little black notepads. The maths didn't matter anymore.

Behind them a building site had popped up in the corner of the llama field. A huge barn and Polster's llama wool factory were under construction. To the side was a state-of-the-art training pitch, with some of the tastiest, lushest grass a llama could ever wish for. On the other side of the road an extension was being built on the side of the farm. This would soon become the Llama United offices where Frank, Monica, Molly and Beetroot would help run the club. Even McCloud had a little place he could call his own: a small caravan parked behind the training pitch. He'd never liked living in houses, so this was perfect for him.

'It's been an amazing season hasn't it?' said Cairo through a mouthful of hot marshmallow.

'You could say that,' replied Tim. 'I don't think I could ever have dreamed this kind of thing would happen.'

'Do you know what's going to happen next?' asked Cairo, accidentally setting fire to his stick.

'I think McCloud is talking to a few people about getting us into a league or the European Cup, but I've got my sights on something bigger.'

'Oh yeah,' said Cairo. 'Like what?'

'Well, next year is a big year in football. A massive, *massive* year.'

Cairo sighed. 'How many times have I told you . . . I still don't know anything about football.'

'It's a World Cup year,' said Tim, with a grin. 'And I think our llamas are ready to take on the world.'

'Ha, ha,' said Cairo, loading three marshmallows on to his stick. 'You're a funny one, Tim. The World Cup . . . funny.'

'You don't know what that is, do you?' asked Tim.

'Not a clue,' replied Cairo. 'But it sounds very far-fetched.'

Tim shook his head and gazed deeply into the fire. 'It's no joke, Cairo,' he said, intently. 'If Arthur Muckluck won the World Cup, then so can our llamas.'

Suddenly the three marshmallows on Cairo's stick burst into neon pink flames so bright that the friends had to shield their eyes.

'Ooh, a spooky sign,' cooed Cairo, 'like what they have in films.'

'Perhaps it is . . . perhaps it is,' replied Tim with a broad smile.

So there you have it. The story of Llama United. Of course, none of this would ever had happened had it not been for *my* incredible football skills. Let's hope the boys remember that. I'd quite like my own statue, even if it is in a field of llamas. After all, football legends have to start somewhere . . .

LEGEND

ACKNOWLEDGEMENTS

Big thanks to:

My superstar agent Gemma Cooper. Her outstanding advice helped me shape the book into what it is today.

Everyone at Macmillan who made me feel so welcome, especially my brilliant editors Rachel Kellehar and Lucy Pearse. Not forgetting Rachel's son Rory, who no doubt helped with Rachel's brainwaves before he entered the world.

My wife Gwen. The book would still be aimlessly wandering about my head, making fart noises, without her words of encouragement.

My sons Spike and Zach, mum Rosie, sister Zoe and cat Pablo – who still hasn't worked out that I don't need a steady stream of dead rodents to help me write.

Friends Guy, Meg, Mike, Ben and three Simons,

who were brilliant at keeping a secret and offering kind words of support.

The football industry, which has shaped my world since the age of five. Despite my cynicism and ridiculous football-related mood swings, I would be a very different person without it (sorry everyone).

Finally to my dad, who passed away when I was editing the first draft. Dad was foolish enough to take me to my first match when I was very small. I caught the football bug that day and couldn't keep away.

C'mon you Irons.

ABOUT THE AUTHOR

Scott Allen was brought up in the horse-racing town of Epsom. After discovering he was too tall and heavy to be a jockey, he turned his attention to football. At sixteen he started writing for fanzines before becoming a professional sports writer, editor and digital-content specialist. He is a West Ham supporter, but we don't hold that against him. Scott now lives in Yorkshire with his wife, two children and cat. He likes Twiglet sandwiches, and still has ambitions of becoming a pirate or an outlaw. *Llama United* is his first novel.

ABOUT THE ILLUSTRATOR

Sarah Horne grew up in snowy Derbyshire, UK, with some goats and a brother.

Alongside working on some very funny children's titles, Sarah has also worked on commissions for the *Guardian*, the *Sunday Times*, Kew Gardens, *Sesame Street* and for IKEA as their Children's Illustrator In Residence.

She now draws, paints, writes and giggles from underneath a pile of paper at her studio in London.